# The Good, Good Sheriff
# &
# Other Voices

*as recorded by*

Joe Vernetti

Copyright © 2006 by Joe Vernetti

ISBN  0-7414-3191-2

*Published by:*

**INFI(∞)ITY**
PUBLISHING.COM

*1094 New DeHaven Street, Suite 100*
*West Conshohocken, PA 19428-2713*
*Info@buybooksontheweb.com*
*www.buybooksontheweb.com*
*Toll-free  (877) BUY BOOK*
*Local Phone (610) 941-9999*
*Fax  (610) 941-9959*

*Printed in the United States of America*

*Printed on Recycled Paper*

*Published  June 2006*

*For Suzie . . .*
       *and Buddy . . .*
              *and Checkers . . .*

*"The thing I care most deeply about?  Oh, I don't know. . ."*

I'm stalling.  Of course I know, but how can I tell her.  Why would I tell her?  Maybe she's just fishing.  Maybe she just wants to feel special ~ you know, loved.

"The thing I care most deeply about?" I repeat, as I gently brush the hair back from the base of her neck.

". . . right now, that would be you."

I'm lying.  Of course I'm lying; but just look at her profiled seductive little smile shimmer into a twinge of seriousness.

Okay focus.  Massage her back with oil.

Less than four hours ago she was an unknown, floating smile.  It was that smile which first captured me.  Maybe I should have let it sail past as a sudden glance.

More oil.

Too much.  Look how perfectly the small of her back pinpoints itself into perfection.  I always did love white lace.  I need more light.  I can barely see her face through these shadows.  But that's okay.  Or is it?  Is a face important in the face of such matters.  "In the face of such matters?"  Oh god, did I mutter that aloud.  Where do I come up with these thoughts?

"This feels wonderful," she's murmuring through the distance. Maybe she heard the face comment thing!  She's murmuring through the distance?  Why do I always think in dialogue, like I'm writing a cheesy private-eye novel?  Well, not always. . .

"Mmmmmm. . ." now she's squirming beneath my hands like a maggot freshly hatched.  Gross; I hate it when I think too much. What the hell, go ahead ~ squirm.  Gives me an opportunity for more light.  Lean forward.  There.  Now slightly brush her lips to

1

yours. Good. On the way back, I'll reach to let up the window shade. It's a good thing the moon is out else there'd be no light at all.

Shade's up.

Alright; I need to focus.

I do miss my old alarm clock though, illuminating its brighter than usual green florescent charm. It was kinda romantic I think. No need for shade trickery there ~ no sir. Just an unpretentious, ever present, bright green glow.

Oh god, she's rolling over. Not yet. No. Push on her shoulder you fool. There. Now rub one hand down her spine. There, strong fingers splitting the back bone on the way down like sealing a Zip Lock bag.

"Your turn," she's saying.

My turn? I'm not even sure I want you here. My turn! Just lay there a second and let me work this out.

"Oh, I don't think so," I reply. "I've just started on your turn." My turn?

The toes . . .

. . . that's it, I'll work the ole toe-foot thing. That always ends up somewhere north of the inner-thigh. White lace city. Jesus, look at me. Sure she's beautiful. Sure she has a killer body; but, don't they all. Well, not all. The ones I date do. Or did. God, look at me: playing a college game at thirty-one.

I can't do this. I can't. But I am. My fingers are sliding down the curve of her hamstring. And I do believe that it is I who just slid further down this very bed to do the old toe-foot thing. God I'm sick.

Rub.

This isn't sick. Everybody does it. Everybody? Well, not everybody; I'm ruling the Pope out on this one.

There. Left leg bent back upon itself. Sole of the foot exposed. Sole of the foot exposed? Sole of the foot exposed; I should write that down. Why is my hand frozen upon her calf, holding her left leg bent upwards. Upwards to expose the sole.

More oil.

I can't reach the bottle without letting go of her leg. Then I'll have to lower the foot. Sole no longer exposed. Then maybe she'll roll over and I'll have to look full upon her. Have to admit she's real ~ that this is real. Okay, so it's real. So what?

Oil damn it, focus . . .

2

. . . I'll use some from her back. Hand frozen on calf. Sole still exposed. There. Right hand rub up and down the spine.

Tingles doesn't it _ _ _ _ _ ? Jesus, I forgot her name. Good thing I didn't say that out loud. I didn't, did I? No. Wait, she's asleep. She's fallen asleep. Rub back down the spine; two fingers opposite each other from the ridge bone downward. There's that smile.

"Ohmmmm," she finally says.

I'll wait for more. I'll wait for words.

Silence. Curse the silence and the moonlight on an auburn-haired beauty laid breast down on my bed.

Oil.

Right, oil. My hand is coated. Good. Sole still exposed. Good. Rub it from the heel upwards, thumb first. There. Never enough pressure.

Toes.

Okay, here we go toes. Separate one by one. Big one first. Surround it deep at the base. Two fingers encircled. Two fingers around one toe. Good. Now pull up. Slide but pull too; kind of a tug wouldn't you say? Why, yes I would. There.

"Ohmmmm . . ."

I'm in. Nine more toes and one last sole and I'm in. But where? White lace city you butt-head. Oh yeah.

Focus.

On what? Her? A smile; a few dances; beer out of my pocket? For what: moonlight on white lace? Every man's fantasy right. But is it? I don't know every man. I don't know any man.

Both hands on the foot work the ankle. There. Now lay it down, gently. Right palm cautiously halfway up the inner-thigh.

"Ohmmmm . . ."

At least she's alive. Good. Five more toes and one last sole. Then not so half way. No sir; five more toes and one last sole then it's white lace city. I should write that too; there's a poem there, I think.

Leg up. Bent towards itself. Second sole exposed. The last sole. I've never really looked at moonlight on white lace. Least not with auburn hair anyway. Never studied it, not really. Casually maybe. How many years since my last auburn? More than a couple. What was her name?

Focus.

One more little toe then the ankle twist thing and . . .

. . . Sandy. No, not Sandy ~ Sally. Yes, Sally. Almost certainly Sally but surely not Sandy. She was blonde; no wait, was there a Sandy?

Focus damn it ~ the ankle twist thing.

Fuck the ankle twist thing. I could do the ankle twist thing blindfolded; that's how much I've done the ankle twist thing. It's all feel anyway.

How many times have I done the ankle twist thing? One more time for sure. There. Lower the foot. Ease up. There. Left hand smoothly up the right inner-thigh. Contact ~ white lace.

Right hand up the back softly. No pressure. There. Brush away hair from the base of her neck.

Nude neck . . .

. . . give it a kiss. Keep lace contact. Don't lose white lace contact. Come on baby; show me a sign. Another gentle kiss? Okay, one more but that's it; on the cheek this time. There.

She's asleep. She's asleep; moonlight on white lace and she's asleep. Who sleeps through the toe-foot thing?

Roll over into the V-support, head in hand, elbow lean. There. She's asleep; she really is. I can't believe it. What time is it. Oh god, I can't believe I just let my left hand rub my eyes. It's coated with oil.

Holy shit, now I've got oil on my face. In my eyes. Left hand? I lost contact. White lace gone. Shit. But she's asleep. I can regain. But she's asleep; there's no sport in that. I could kiss her awake.

What time is it? The dim red glow of the new alarm clock says 3:56. Four o'clock. Oh man, I should be asleep. Lay down. She's got the pillow. Well then, stay in the V-support head in hand thing. I can't. Wake her up then. Left hand fingers invert to stroke the length of her back. I'm watching them move slowly down the gentle curve of her pinpointed waist.

Contact.

Retrieve.

I can't do this. I don't know her.

She doesn't know me. Thirty-one years. That's 365 days times thirty-one. That's . . . that's . . .

Well that's a lot. We could fall in love. Who wouldn't fall in love with auburn and white lace in the moonlight; but, she'd never truly know about all those lumped together 365 days. Never truly. She doesn't even know I have a new alarm clock.

Gotta pee.

Great, now what?  Get up stupid - go pee.  Gentle kiss on the shoulder.  Roll over.  There.  Escape.

Can't.  Can't pee; she'll hear.  She'll wake up.  Then what?  My turn!  Yeah right.  Go downstairs.  Pee downstairs.

Good, now flush.  Can't.  Gotta flush.  Flush.

A drink of water then back upstairs.  Shit that's bright.  Why so bright?  It's three cubic feet of space and they're lighting a fucking parking lot.  Look, a zit.  Perfect, a zit smack in the middle of my hairless chest.  Good thing I left my pants on; lord knows what's growing on my butt.

There.  No more bright.  No more zit.

Man, my throat's dry.

Drink the water stupid.  The cap's too tight.  Too tight?  It's just wet ~ squeeze; now twist.  There.  That sure is a loud crackling plastic safety cap seal being broken noise.  I think it's echoing.

Oh . . .

. . . another sip.

That feels good.  How much beer did I have?  Four maybe.  Maybe five?  It's been hours.

Bright light.

No.  Take the bottle stupid, in case she's awake.

Darkness.

A little stall, moment alone.

Let's see what's worth learning on *The Learning Channel*.  Volume . . .

Volume . . .

Jesus, where's the volume ~ she'll wake up for sure.

**Mute** in big blue letters across the screen.  In case you are, I guess.  No, that's not right.  You'd have to be deaf to need blue letters.  Mute?  The television's mute.  I get it.  Man, I'm tired.  Oh look, Roman architecture just discovered the arch.  Thought they did that last week.  No matter: click.  Now it's mute and blind.  No, that's not right.

Silence.

Bless the dark silence.  Oh, how did this couch get so soft?  Wait; no, there's a blanket under me.  I'm laying on a soft blanket.  No, correct that, I'm laying under a soft blanket.  This feels good; like I'm back home good.  Just for a second though.  Then I'll go back up to white lace.

Light.

5

Sunlight? Just a little though. Only just enough to erase the gray shadows from the room. Oh shit ~ white lace and moonlight! This water feels warm. This plastic's luke warm. The water must be too. Clock on the stove says seven forty-three. That means it's six forty-three; or, maybe eight forty? No six. Definitely six forty-three. New water. New crackling plastic safety cap as I ascend the stairs. Hey, that's pretty good. New plastic safety cap as I ascend the stairs . . .

I'm humming along . . .

I'm humming along to an inner-voice refrain of: new crackling plastic safety cap? I must be tired. I am tired but there's this thing on my bed. This auburn-haired, white-laced thing.

The sunlight, not yet full. It's found her lower legs. Soon to engulf her. Shade down.

Quietly, damn it.

Water bottle on night stand. Hey, there's my magazine. I could have read. God, she's beautiful with her left leg pulled up into her belly like that. Just high enough to alter the accent of white lace and expose the soft under-curve of a finely-shaped left breast, only slightly.

Look. She's sleeping on folded hands. Bet that'll leave an impression. More than I have, that's for sure. I could wake her. One little kiss then I'd leave an impression. I can't wake her now. I gotta find a way to stay out of that bed.

I know, I'll write. I may be just tired enough to create. Some of my best stuff this way. Maybe I'll chance upon the one great story. Clean paper; clear desk; new roller-ball pen; there. No, not there. Why do I always write? I don't even like to write; well sometimes . . .

Flow damn it.

Just some simple words. Okay:

> *they're simple words*
> *their simple words*

Cross that out.

Next.

I said next.

High school.

High school?

Why should I write of high school?

Because we were tigers . . . Okay, what of it . . .

Tigers?  Yes, tigers:

> *dread beasts, tigers*
> *dead poets, liars*
> *one tears apart*
> *one eats the heart*
>
> *this the point*
> *i wish to make*
> *for you to anoint*
> *by which you take*
>
> *dread beast, tiger*
> *dead poet, liar*

It needs a title.  Titles should flow . . . Don't force titles. . .

Wait.  One will come:

### *A Tiger's Tale*

There.  I'll call it *A Tiger's Tale*.

She's curled around the whole bed now.  But I need sleep.  I could spoon her.  But could I?  I know me.  I'd spoon two, maybe three minutes then:  contact.  Either tit or white lace, no matter. Contact is contact.  Then this whole night of staying away - of being good - is wasted.  I just can't bare to catch up another soul on the past thirty-one years.  It's all over for me.  The game is up.

*A Tiger's Tale*.  I like it.  It'd make a good epitaph.  I need sleep. Not the deep sleep, just a little sleep.  Maybe I don't have to spoon. There's enough room to just lay down next to auburn and white lace.

7

I can do this.  What time is it ~ 7:13.  A red 7:13, who could get used to that?  Head back around.  Now just ease onto a corner of the pillow.  There, see.  I can do this.  Now steady.  Okay, maybe just a little spoon ~~~

~~~~~ Contact.

## The Curse of Jonesy's Gold ~

Rising from the black swamp around me, ghosts hide in plain sight as a fog billows beneath them. They speak a spectral voice. Still, some confuse these nightly voices for wind blown air weeping through the hollows of mysterious trees. Aye, these trees draped in hairy moss appear to be of the devil's garden but, if it be the wind, where goeth the fog? I walk again my walk of sorrow and shame on this night. I lay witness to a stillness in the fog on this night, as true of many nights before. The air is as still as the breath of Christ; and, yet, the haunts repeat. They repeat and repeat and repeat. "Jonesy," they call through the calm. "Jonesy; Jonesy; Jonesy~~~"

I dare not answer. I dare not answer lest they confuse me for Jonesy, these many years deceased. Some say me touched. Some swear a frightful oath on the common bible that these calling voices be but the wind lurching its way to the sea. Aye, it may be a searching wind. But it be a spectral wind, to be sure, for I am among the few who know it to be tracing to where we lost Jonesy. Jonesy was not lost to us in body, you see. No, not in body, but the sea surely kept his soul. We carried his body with us to the shore; each in our own way.

I alone hear the spectral voices calling Jonesy's soul homeward. Surely now the ghosts have gathered in numbers; surely they have gathered his many parts that we laid in waste along the shore. Their numbers speak. Maybe through the trees; maybe through the fog; maybe through the wind as an instrument; but, it is surely God's wind ~ created by the sweep of his angry hand.

We put to sea with twenty-eight souls aboard. We put to sea with a promise of half pay at Boston Towne and a share of the the profits upon safe harbour a year and six hence. It was not to be. We did not put in at Boston Towne. We loaded cargo by the nets. We loaded cargo from the barges that lay in wait of our arrival. The captain had announced the port full. The captain had said a great many things not of whole truth. I think captains should not hide in their cabins when the news is bad. Our captain left us opportunity to speak freely with the barge men on that black day. They told of an easy passage to the port. They spoke of empty berths and of fine public houses. The barge men even spoke tales of loose women to be had. They'd had questions of their own. They queried of our delay? Those Boston men told of waiting with loaded barges three days and nights for our arrival.

We were assumed not to be men of wit and learning. Aye, but we sure knew of a scandal when one arose. Many of the twenty-eight had worked the barges. Many of the twenty-eight could reason an advance knowledge of the captain and his officers. We were never to put in at Boston Towne was the speculation and I slowed to agree. The devil was dancing with a dagger around my heart in those moments of calm. He is a fine temptress when he smells fresh bait in the waters between heaven and hell.

I pulled at the hempt ropes until my hands bled on that day. Others stopped pulling and pushing and prying the cargo aboard. Others demanded half pay. Others shouted mutinous words as they drank more than their daily grog. These numbered thirteen of the twenty-eight. Jonesy was not aboard. He had been sent ashore with dispatches and there was speculation as to where his sympathies would lie. Jonesy was borne to the sea. Jonesy would know the right and the wrong of it. I determined to wait. I determined to watch and do my duty as sworn. A bargain the captain had struck, yes. The other part of that bargain my father had struck on my behalf and my boyish mind was ill-prepared to break either man's word. Jonesy would determine the course and tack to take so I pulled and tugged and sweated blood from my hands as I paid penance for the thirteen.

I can still feel the fibers of those ropes brushing my open wounds on these damp and foggy nights. I can still hear the echoes of protest and the drunken debates of the thirteen as the captain hid behind cabin doors. He was aware. The captain must have been in knowledge of the thirteen for that folly quickly ceased when Young

Carter jumped ship in an attempt to stow on the last departing barge. The guard was quickly called and their shots rang out. Why were their weapons charged? I have often pondered the guard's preparedness for the troubles of the thirteen. I often conclude that the captain had expected riotous behavior. The figures in this dark and foggy swamp agree. Their spectral voices posture but one answer: the captain knew. It was a sickening sight to see those bullets pierce the building seas as Young Carter dove beneath the waves. The thirteen grew in number then. The thirteen impressed two more into their ranks as they were herded below decks under the threat of fresh powder and shot.

One can theory as to the captain's mind before the smoke billowed from those guns. One need not speculate on the aftermath. One need not ponder his mind nor the clearness of his directive. Rations were cut for the fifteen to water alone. Their half pay promised to the guard. The half pay of fifteen divided by four. I reasoned then it best I had waited for Jonesy's return. The captain's officers and the four and then the fifteen. Young Carter was gone to his fate. That left three awaiting Jonesy. Three of twenty-seven swinging from the balance of right and wrong. Swinging between loyalty and the gallows of mutiny and shame.

Jonesy rowed slow towards the afterdeck. His years sensed trouble. The first mate made fast the line and climbed aboard but Jonesy delayed. Where were the twenty-eight? Where be the captain awaiting news from ashore? Questions danced through Jonesy's eyes as I studied the every move of his return. Ropes were made fast and the skiff pulled up with Jonesy still aboard. O'Hearn got to him first, while he was still seated ahold of the skiff. Though O'Hearn preceded my approach, Jonesy's eyes didn't change. They kept the erie black calm of a seer who knows of things unspoken.

I see him as he was then through this damp, still fog. I hear the swamp frogs and voices in the night only as a backdrop to the darkness shown through Jonesy in that moment and I know, as I have known these many years, that he was of a mind to cut the ropes. His thoughts were to flee back to Boston Towne and be done with the whole affair. I dare say I am responsible for staying his plan. I live that moment nightly as I see him reach for his knife, his bone-handled knife that my father presented to him on his thirty-fifth birthday. I should not have caught Jonesy's eye. I should have looked away and allowed his escape.

11

I was making way across the rolling deck. I was making my way to Jonesy's side when the orders came to make sail. The first mate barked orders to continue our plan for The Horn with, or without, the fifteen. "China awaits our cargo and riches await our ship," was his shout. "Make sail," his repeated command. I stepped onward. I closed on Jonesy but his searing eyes sent me to the ropes. He motioned me to my duties. I was his charge. I was an oath he swore to my dear mother and father and I obeyed.

We made sail against a good wind that late afternoon. Jonesy worked the riggings like a song. His was beauty in motion. He sensed my nerves. Jonesy felt the wings of the ship as she swayed into the darkening night and he calmed me with action. I was assigned to the watch at the forecastle before my lips could speak my many questions; yet, Jonesy's eyes twinkled a soothing reply to unspoken words. I believed those telling eyes and I again obeyed. In silence, I obeyed as I heard the moanings and cursings of the fifteen rising from amongst the cargo.

I heard many a familiar voice rise but none so familiar as Jonesy's as the fog began to sweep across our bow. I left my watch to creep closer to the knowledge of Jonesy's voice. I left my duty in fear of discovery by the guard but I thirsted to know our fate. I thirsted to hear Jonesy's take on the matters of that day. He spoke of deception. He had rowed the first mate ashore not with dispatches but with the captain's ready cash. Jonesy was kept in secret from this knowledge but had many a friend in Boston Towne give him the sorry news of the captain being denied credit for the cargo. Jonesy discovered that our half pay went towards a bond on the cargo which had awaited our arrival.

I faintly heard the beginnings of a plan being hatched when the rattle of the guard's sword sent me fearfully to my post. It was as foggy a night as this night save for the moss and the snakes and the trees. Spectral voices were calling Young Carter home through the fog of that night. I fell asleep to the swooshing sound of bullets racing through remembered waves as their threat of death traced towards that poor boy's heart.

Morning beat hard on the decks of that fateful ship. A dead calm was upon the crew as morning came reluctantly through the thickening fog and sails were ordered to be stowed. I awoke safe. I awoke under a blanket in my hammock. I was not to learn until later that Jonesy had carried me to my rest and had stood watch alone the entire night. I was later to learn a great many things. I was never near enough to Jonesy to ask my many questions. I awakened to the sound of prisoners being led in threes to the upper decks. I laid cowardly under my blanket in fear and confusion. Roaring questions rocked my hammock in the callous calm of that sea. Should I have been one of the fifteen? Should I now stand their ground?

I arose to seek Jonesy. Yet, in a shameful pause, I awaited for the last of the fifteen to pass. I followed them to their fate as the captain mustered the crew to read their punishment. I found Jonesy too late. I found Jonesy already summoned to the base of the quarterdeck as the captain handed him a whip. The captain ordered Jonesy to lash each of the fifteen thirty times about the bare back. The captain was testing Jonesy's loyalties. The captain knew. Yes, the captain knew that as Jonesy went so went the crew.

Dirty Johnson was to be the first. He was tied to the mainmast as Jonesy approached him with tender steps. When Jonesy got near enough he bent to whisper something into Dirty Johnson's ear. "Stick to the plan," he was reported to have said. "Stick to the plan." Jonesy then straightened into as proud a pose as any man has yet to muster. I saw a smile grow onto Dirty Johnson face as Jonesy turned to face the captain. From my view, Dirty Johnson's smile bent clear around that mainmast.

Jonesy pressed the butt end of the whip defiantly towards the captain as he announced, "You do it. On your honor, sir, you whip these cheated and innocent men." The captain had his answer. The captain knew that his command would be lost to him if he did not reply in kind. The guards with lowered, loaded pistols awaited the captain's reply. His three officers awaited the captain's reply. The fifteen awaited with freshening hope in this silent pause. Tense were the three who remained on the outskirts of this folly: myself and O'Hearn and Timothy Peters. All waited as Jonesy stood firm, whip held aloft.

Reply he did. The captain replied with force and vigor. Jonesy was grabbed up by the guard and tied opposite Dirty Johnson, their hands lashed together with rope around the mainmast. I dare say that Dirty Johnson's smile eroded into Jonesy's stare. I wonder these many dark nights away at how it must have felt being so close to Jonesy's eyes as the guard beat him and beat him and beat him about the head. I often foolishly feel deep into these dark swamp waters with the hope of being bitten by some mysterious creature so that I might feel some of Jonesy's pain as I see again and again the lash of that whip peel the skin from his back and legs.

As a boy, I could bear no more. As a boy just put to sea, I could witness no more of this cruelty of man upon man and I acted a fool. I rushed the guard and tried to pull away the whip but I was hurled backwards. I rushed again as another guard interceded and, in our struggle, he discharged his loaded pistol. The shot pierced the captain's face and he fell instantly over the railing of the quarterdeck. He fell amongst the fifteen. The battle raged from that point to a fury of bodies and knives and blood and shot. I do not recall, even to this night, the blow that ended my part in the fray. I remember well, have you, the aftermath. I remember well awakening next to Jonesy's oozing flesh in the captain's berth.

His breathing was a harsh thing to hear and I jumped quickly to my feet in the belief that I had been killed. I thought myself to be in the fresh throes of the devil's parlor. I had not recognized the moving, breathing ooze as Jonesy in the moment of my awakening. I imagined him to surely be the first phase of my eternity of torture. I walk this swamp at night wishing upon wishes that it had been so. Had I only been one of the lucky to have been killed in that frightful battle, had I only perished, I would not be cursed with this ability to hear the spectral voices calling through the trees for Jonesy's return.

No longer were the fifteen. No longer were the guards and the officers. Thrown overboard were the bodies of many. The ship of twenty-eight housed only twelve upon my awakening. Eight of the fifteen had survived, Dirty Johnson in their numbers. The other two reluctant outsiders, O'Hearn and Timothy Peters, survived as well. I was soon to learn that even they were to be fated a death at sea. Soon I was to learn a great many things; most importantly, I learned to fear the eight that remained.

I looked frantically about the captain's cabin; in hopes of what, I do not know. I looked about and in and around but I dared not look upon Jonesy. I could not look upon Jonesy's melting flesh. The stench suggested we had been bedded for days. Smells slowly came to my awakening senses that I dare not recall. They drifted about the room until every corner was filled with the stench of putrid, dying flesh. Jonesy's flesh. Had ours been a fine ship, a ship of the Line, the captain's cabin would have had many options for fresh air. The captain's cabin would have had private privys and wide windows of glass and hinges. Our ship had no such luxuries.

The captain's cabin had but two tiny portholes with fixed glass for light.

I ventured out of closed doors then in search of breathable air. I stumbled with throbbing head onto the open quarterdeck and was blinded by the brightness of day. Braxton Gates caught me as I began to teeter from the dizziness of it all. I was glad of it. Had I fallen, I do not think I would have had the strength to regain my feet. They would surely have returned me to Jonesy's side. Braxton Gates settled me to the railing so that I might regain my own posture. I steadied myself with weak arms and looked slowly about.

Our sails were full in the stiff breeze as we sailed speedily towards deeper waters. The sea was choppy but not so as to rattle the ships rigging beyond a whisper. My eyes were slow to adjust to the sun. It was another minute before I saw the horror of Timothy Peters and O'Hearn hanging by the wrists from ropes tied to the beam of our lowermost sail, their feet missing the deck by nearly a foot. This, I was to learn, was the doings of Tommy Franklin. He had won over the opinion of the eight. He reasoned that Peters and O'Hearn could not be trusted with their secrets once a port was decided upon. Franklin had even wished to link me to Timothy Peters and O'Hearn. He had wished for me their fate but, this, the eight would not allow.

Tommy Franklin had reasoned that we three should meet the same end as the many for we had not joined the fifteen from the first. Our lives rested upon Jonesy. The eight voted to await the trusted opinion of Jonesy on this and other matters. I had been spared from hanging from the rigging by my having been but a boy, a boy entrusted to the care of the respected Jonesy.

Thus, was my day of freedom. That night the drunkenness came. That night of bright moon and stars saw the end of O'Hearn and Timothy Peters. The devil danced a four-step beat that night. The devil was presented a stage awash in fresh blood and flesh. Tommy Franklin was the first to draw his sword and begin the torment of Peters and O'Hearn. Tommy Franklin was the first to dance about their feet. He was the first to poke at their ribs and their manly parts with the sharp tip of a sword. He was not to be the last. Our numbers were shrinking as the devil counted his toll. The eight were entranced by a euphoric freedom from God's threat of justice. Their fates had been sealed with the deaths of the officers and the guards. The eight knew that hell awaited the end of their mortal souls. Nothing can stop such men; nothing remains to hold their base elements in check.

Timothy Peters was the first to be run through. He hung there swaying in the rigging like a bag of grain awaiting a miller's wagon. He hung there for O'Hearn to ponder as the night rolled slowly on and the devil danced a new dance of joy. I did not witness O'Hearn's final demise. Dirty Johnson whisked me away from those sights with these few words of caution, "They are of a like mind towards you lad. They have fears that Jonesy will not recover and believe us wasting time." With those words, Dirty Johnson stowed me away in the captain's cabin for safer keeping. He forbade me to go back out onto the deck and its open air.

I would sooner drown in the slime-crusted waters of this swamp than to go back to the memory of that cabin; yet, I do go back. I often see those following three days as haunting memories but they were mere preludes to future events. All was not despair. There were moments of hope in that cabin. Hope that Jonesy would awaken and finally answer my many questions. Hope, with every moan of the ship, that the door was opening to the want of fresh supplies of food and water. Hope for a mother's warm bosom and caressing hand.

These things were not to be had. Dirty Johnson remembered me on the second day. He brought fresh water and some hard tack but only slipped them through the crack of a partially opened door. I pressed the water to Jonesy's lips with the aid of a soaked rag. I had hoped some of that moist giver of life to be passing his lips but I could not be sure. I still could not bring myself to touch the mass that had once been Jonesy. I was barely surviving the stench; the putrid stench of Jonesy's rotting flesh in the stale cabin air. I dare say that these nightly swamp gases smell of rose petals washed in fresh dew compared to that foulness.

It came to me then that Tommy Franklin may well have sized the situation correctly. I began to hear Jonesy's increasingly coarse breathing as a sign that I was soon to be alone. I tried to reason as Jonesy would have reasoned. I tried to plan for losing the safety of his shield. I needed a weapon; of that, I was certain. I could see the tip of Jonesy's bone-handled knife peering out of the top of his belt. I could see the tip of that knife for sure; but, it was solidly wedged between his body and the back wall of the captain's berth and, as I have said, my young mind was still not of the sort to move Jonesy or to touch him in any way.

I began to look about the cabin in earnest. I pried open cabinets and drawers in search of a weapon. It had appeared that the captain had taken all of his arms with him to the fight and to his death. I never found a weapon in that cabin. No, nor did I look further once I found the gold. Sixteen pieces of Spanish gold lay hidden in the false bottom of one of the captain's drawers and I snatched them up. Of a sudden, I had the cold power of gold in my young hands.

New feelings swept over me then. I had seen gold but one time before. A gentleman had stopped at my father's house to inquire about buying one of father's prized horses. Those few steeds were near all that father had left. His horses were lone remembrances of the days before our financial ruin; and, he would not sell. The man said he had ready cash as he pulled many a fine gold piece from his purse; yet, father could not be swayed. He would not sell. The man raised his sum. Father refused. As the offer soared even higher, I saw father look into my mother's eyes. He never spoke a word to the man. Father never spoke a word. He simply fetched up the horse in question and exchanged it for the gold.

I had often dreamed of the power behind that man's gold. Now I had my own. It was not a theft, I reasoned. I set it in my mind that Spanish gold could be of little use to a dead captain. I reasoned that gold, mind you, would be of great use to Jonesy and me should a need arise. I closed the false bottom of that drawer and sat crossed legged on that cabin floor. I played with my gold for hours. I stacked that gold long ways and sideways as I dreamed of fine houses and of large private meals. I dreamed the many dreams of a boy as those coins rolled from hand to hand along the cabin floor. Only the coming dark of night stopped my play.

I grew ever more fearful of the eight as darkness descended upon my gold. Its changing effects had begun. I began to worry that the eight would soon decide to plunder the captain's cabin. I foresaw them finding my gold. I had to hide the freshly found treasure. But where? If a boy could find a secret drawer then where could the gold be safe? That's when Jonesy moaned. He moaned an opportune and deep moan, not unlike the sounds of them that lurk in the shadows of this black swamp.

It took me near half the night to whittle a proper needle from the splinters I carved out of the captain's desk. Truth be known, it first took me near an hour to work the courage to reach for Jonesy's bone-handled knife. Once in hand, I set it to motion. I fashioned me a needle and I tore some thread from a rip in Jonesy's britches.

That gold was changing me for sure because I no longer looked upon Jonesy as a pile of rotting flesh. I no longer saw Jonesy as the dear friend of my father. I looked upon Jonesy then as but a hiding place for my gold. I did not bother with smells or peeling flesh. I knew the waist of Jonesy's britches to be a safe place to hide the gold and I sewed the sixteen pieces into its seam. When all was set, I sprawled out onto the cabin floor and dreamed of exotic ports. I rolled around as the images danced through me like fairies in a poem. Yes, my gold bought a wealth of dreams on that night.

I awoke on the morning of the third day to a poke. I awoke to the stare of Dirty Johnson's rotten teeth. He and Braxton Gates had overheard Tommy Franklin's plan to murder me and Jonesy on that very night. Dirty Johnson whispered, "Tommy boy won over the others so six against two would it be. No fair measure of success could be had in such a fight." It was early morning and the other six were still sleeping off their drunkenness while Dirty Johnson and Braxton Gates had come to a plan of their own. Dirty Johnson had no cause to do me ill. Dirty Johnson had no equal cause to come to my aid but he was surely in Jonesy's debt. He surely owed Jonesy and he spoke as much as he and Braxton Gates heaved Jonesy's mass between them and dragged him off to the skiff. I worried openly to God that they might discover my gold as Jonesy slipped continuously from their grasp.

We made the skiff undetected and Dirty Johnson left us to gather supplies of food and water. Braxton Gates helped me settle Jonesy into the bow of the skiff as he explained how the others would be told. For a moment, Braxton Gates paused his speech as he eyed Jonesy slip off the bow seat of the skiff. I still hear that gold jingle and sing to this day as it echoes across time. I had sewn them in separate and, to this day, I do not know which two of the sixteen pieces touched but Braxton Gates surely paused before speaking of how I would be thought to have secreted off with Jonesy in the middle of the night. Dirty Johnson and Braxton Gates were of no mind to get into that skiff and set themselves adrift in the wide Atlantic. That was not their plan. There were a great many plans to go astray on the fateful ship of twenty-eight. A great many plans indeed.

Braxton Gates was lowering the skiff with me and Jonesy aboard when we first heard Dirty Johnson's cries. Dirty Johnson's screams echoed closer and closer as he ran to where the lowered skiff had been. Braxton Gates had heard better those callings, those telling screams. Dirty Johnson's words echoed towards the water in a jumble of confusion as they mingled with other sounds and I was left to wonder. I wondered if the six had discovered my absence. I wondered if maybe one of the six had known of the gold and was coming to claim my sixteen pieces of treasure. I even began to reason that Dirty Johnson had known. I wondered if he had had designs on that gold and had cleared me out of the cabin so that he might lay his own claim to the prize.

Yes, Braxton Gates had heard better Dirty Johnson's cry. Braxton Gates had had little time to wonder. As he witnessed Dirty Johnson in flight from the six, Braxton Gates dove into the sea. It appears that Dirty Johnson had been discovered trying to steal food for me and Jonesy. In his haste, Dirty Johnson had awoken the six to our planned escape. As Dirty Johnson later would tell, he had hoped to battle the six in the confines of the afterdeck. Dirty Johnson had had brave plans to corner the six with the aid of Braxton Gates. As it were, Dirty Johnson followed Braxton Gates into the sea.

With two in the sea and two more in the skiff, the twenty-eight had dwindled to six. We had put to sea with twenty-eight souls aboard and a promise of half pay at Boston Towne; yet, the twenty-eight were no more. The doomed ship sped away from our little skiff on that clear, warm morning with but six souls aboard to witness its final days. I have roamed this swamp many a night with stories rolling through my head. I have walked the streets of the nearby village and I have sat in the corner of the tavern. I have listened these many years for news of the twenty-eight. High tales have come my way but none ring so true as the burning. No, none ring so true. They tell of a ship being found burnt to the water line with none but six charred bodies aboard. I do tell that the devil most surely danced a final jig on the decks of that ship. I slip through the darkness now with the knowing that the devil is still tapping a steady beat, awaiting the last of the twenty-eight.

The devil may soon have possession of my soul. He may indeed. But not, I pray, until Jonesy's return. That boy adrift in a small skiff has many an unanswered question for Jonesy. He will have to get his answers through me for I left that small boy behind in those coming days. It may well be that I alone will hear the spectral callings of Jonesy's voice when his soul returns from the sea. I alone await his return.

That skiff indeed seemed a small craft once Dirty Johnson and Braxton Gates were fished from the chilly waters. It was a hard task for a boy my size and I lost one of the oars in the struggle. I had thought of beating them back into the water with that oar. I had thought first of my gold and then of Jonesy and I was of a mind not to help Dirty Johnson and Braxton Gates over the high sides of the skiff. Nay, but the devil and his gold had yet to gain complete custody of my soul so I did not beat them back. I did not sell my soul to the devil on our first day adrift.

They were not long removed from the near fate of drowning in the cold Atlantic before Gates and Johnson became none too happy with their new fate of being adrift at sea with no food nor water. Yes, how soon men forget to thank their maker for gifts when presented. They should have prayed and thanked their God for their safety. They should have prayed, indeed. Prayer might well have brought us together on that little raft. I tell now that they did not pray a thankful prayer. I tell now that they argued with frightful words. Braxton Gates had wanted to drift with the current when he discovered we had but one oar. Braxton Gates had wanted to save his energy and await a passing ship but Dirty Johnson had thought otherwise. Dirty Johnson had thought we should row. One oar or none he insisted we row. Dirty Johnson wanted each to take a turn rowing towards the west in the hope of reaching the colonies.

Our boat measured nine feet from bow to stern and had three seats which were fashioned as benches between the side planks. Jonesy had slipped off of the forward-most seat and had settled with his back against the curve of the bow while his legs from the knees down draped over the seat. Once the struggle of saving Johnson and Gates had ebbed, I brushed Jonesy's legs aside and settled into the port side of that bow seat. Our seat was set back a foot from the curve of the bow while the aft seat was settled directly into the wood of the stern. In the exact center of the boat there remained a few blocks of squared-off wood to constantly remind us where the small mast and sail would be fastened had the captain not had them removed on a previous voyage. You see, that's why the center bench was not in the true center of the skiff. The center seat was positioned a foot closer to the stern than the bow. It should have been a mile away. Little good did that seat do to separate Braxton Gates from Dirty Johnson as he sat facing the seat to the stern.

Braxton Gates and Dirty Johnson struggled for control of our little craft harder than they had struggled for the fateful ship of twenty-eight and with little good effect. They faced each other in the rising, blinding sun and argued both the ills of rowing and of drifting. Braxton Gates finally held our oar aloft and made his case that one oar was a worse fate than none at all. He made his case that that oar would be better tossed after its twin into the sea. Dirty Johnson near upset the small skiff when he first lunged for that swinging oar. Dirty Johnson repeated many a foul word at his friend Braxton Gates as he swept his hands and feet forward in a pattern that allowed him to still balance against the aft seat of the skiff. He should not have spoken such foul words to his friend, I think.

I looked away then from their folly for a brief moment to ensure that Jonesy was still breathing. I was concerned a little for his comfort. I was concerned that the rawness of Jonesy's bare back and legs were being tormented as they scraped against the coarse wood of the skiff with each new motion of the sea. I was concerned for a great many things on that desperate skiff; but, I must now confess here at this spot, as I have confessed a thousand nights before. I must now confess on this alter of Jonesy's bones that I was most concerned for my gold. I was most concerned that the position of Jonesy's body would not split the gold from the seam of his britches. Aye, in my fresh moment of greed, little did I notice as the arguments of Gates and Johnson grew. Little did I notice the rocking of the skiff as Dirty Johnson made a leap for the oar with both hands.

I looked only in time to see Braxton Gates swing the oar overhead and bury it into Dirty Johnson's skull. Dirty Johnson fell instantly over the starboard side of the skiff and began to sink into the black depths of the sea. Only Dirty Johnson's right leg was still visible to me when his friend dove into the sea after him. Braxton Gates grabbed up that leg and, with all his might, righted Dirty Johnson's body to the surface. Faintly can I now imagine how strong Braxton Gates must have been. He had broken the water with only his head and shoulders; yet, he had somewhere found the strength to hold his friend's head aloft while his right arm found the strength to pull this tangled human anchor to the stern of our boat.

Yes, I watched their struggle for life. I watched, unwilling to go to their aid. I watched as Braxton Gates held fast to his friend with his left arm and struggled to pull himself aboard with his right. He failed that first hour. That first hour he called to me in kindness and with pleas of mercy in his voice but I would not help. The second hour Braxton Gates rested. The second hour Braxton Gates looked upon me with hatred and murderous intent. I felt for Jonesy's bone-handled knife many a time that second hour. I ensured many a times that it were still tucked tight inside my belt.

In the third hour Dirty Johnson awoke to their situation. In the third hour Dirty Johnson found the strength to hold himself tight to the stern of the skiff while Braxton Gates completed his own struggle to get aboard. Braxton Gates had used his final strength. Braxton Gates could do little else for his friend through the balance of that first day but to hold to his wrist and keep Dirty Johnson adrift behind the skiff.

God's sun showed little mercy as those next hours passed. God's sun showed little mercy to me and Jonesy as I had shown little mercy to Johnson and Gates. Jonesy's exposed flesh was beginning to burn in the intense sunlight and I could do little to prevent his fresh source of torture. I tried to cool Jonesy with splashes of cold sea water but he struggled mightily against the salt on his wounds. Jonesy had no voice, nor once did he open his eyes, but his body did violently beat back the idea of being cooled with sea water. His thrashing was of such violent nature that I grew once again concerned for the safety of my gold. Aye, the gold. I counseled myself to allow Jonesy's flesh to burn for fear that his thrashing would expose my treasure.

That day passed long as our four doomed souls settled into an erie silence. The skiff fell silent long before night crept upon our strange little crew. I little imagined the struggles of Johnson and Gates as the moon arose full and bright over the sea. I little cared for the pain Braxton Gates must have endured in his struggle to hold his friend fast to the stern of our skiff. I felt only my own thirst and my own hunger. I felt only my own burning skin rub against Jonesy's rotting flesh and cared little for the concerns of Johnson or Gates. The moon arose and the stars settled into the night as I felt again and again for Jonesy's bone-handled knife. I slept in pieces at the beginning of that night. I felt safe from Braxton Gates for he could do little harm to me or Jonesy while he was tied to the struggle of holding onto Dirty Johnson. I felt secure that my gold was safe. Somewhere between the rocking of the sea and the steady noise of Jonesy's breathing, I fell into a deeper sleep than I have since been allowed; and, somewhere in that long night Braxton Gates found the strength to get his friend aboard.

I awoke to the sight of Dirty Johnson astride the length of the center seat. His head was bent against the port side of the skiff. I did not see clearly the dried blood that covered his hair and face until the sun arose in the east. Nor did I see clearly Braxton Gates asleep in the stern seat with our lone oar across his lap. The moon had set early that night and I did not see clearly a great number of signs during the first moments of my awakening. I did not see that the red sky of dawn was a foretelling sky; that the coming day was to be the day I was to say farewell to Jonesy and to my own salvation.

I awoke to a rough sea and to the silence of Jonesy's breathing. Gone was the slow steady rhythm of the skiff and Jonesy's breathing marking time with each other and I feared him dead. I feared him called away from his suffering while I slept a boyish sleep. I should have thought more of Jonesy then but my own thirst and hunger allowed me to think of little else in those last moments of darkness. I thought of little else but my own needs and I did not check over Jonesy's corpse. I did not hold his hand and speak the prayers one should speak at such times. I awaited the sun and I thought only of the new pains that would accompany its bright torturous heat.

Braxton Gates was the first of the pair to awaken. He opened his eyes to the fresh light of seeing his friend's bashed head and he vomited the last of his liquids over the side. I noticed then that he was shivering in a violent way. Braxton Gates was in ill health to be sure. Braxton Gates had struggled hard to save his friend but he awoke to the fear that his struggles had been in vain for Dirty Johnson, sprawled motionless across the center seat, surely looked a dead man. Braxton Gates's first thoughts were to lean towards his friend. Braxton Gates placed his hand over Dirty Johnson's nose to feel for his breathing. That is when he relaxed. Braxton Gates relaxed into the stern seat still shivering enough to gently rock the boat from starboard to port and back.

That rocking continued near an hour but his motion did not upset me as much as his mumbling. Braxton Gates held fast to our oar while he talked to himself in a low and unhearable voice. I see through these many years and I feel the mumbles of Braxton Gates on these damp nights. I feel his low cursings crawl upon my skin in slow waves. They say me touched as I walk from the town and disappear into this swamp when the moon arises. They say me touched because I hear the callings of the spectral voices in this swamp. I dare say those townsfolk have never seen a touched man. I dare say they would not think me touched had they laid witness to Braxton Gates on the morning of our second day adrift. His mumblings grew to a roar as he began to shout to God and to the devil. He began to chant many a chant in favor of his injured friend. He vowed that he had been led by the devil to do harm to Dirty Johnson. He vowed and vowed that he had been wrong. He vowed that he should have agreed to row, and row he did. Braxton Gates became a fever of rowing as he plowed the oar through the water from the port side and then the starboard and then the port and then the starboard. He stood in the aft of our little boat and exhausted himself near three hours with his feverous rowing.

He pulled his anger through the water with that oar and exhausted his remaining strength. Braxton Gates peered in all directions near the end of those blistering hours of rowing; but, the sea still looked wide and relentless. He stood in the aft of that boat a beaten man and he cursed the Lord and the devil. Braxton Gates then cursed his parents and our dead captain and many another soul whom I did not know as he threw our oar to the sea.

All hope drifted away with that oar. All hope that I or my gold would see the riches it could bring floated into the wide Atlantic atop that piece of life saving wood. I thought of Jonesy and of Dirty Johnson then. I envied that they had not witnessed Braxton Gates's madness. I envied that they were not forced to think of our thirst and the heat and the painful deaths which lay ahead. I wanted to be Jonesy then. I wanted to lie idle in the bow of the boat and drift painlessly to the rhythm of the ocean swells. I desired a great many things that late morning but mostly I prayed that I might perish before the heat of the midday found my parched lips.

Dirty Johnson awoke in a fit of madness. Dirty Johnson awoke unaware of his surroundings or our plight. Dirty Johnson saw only the blinding midday sun slowly tracing towards the west. In his prostrate and desperate state, Dirty Johnson could fathom little more. I was more of a mind to pray for Dirty Johnson in the heat of that midday. I had watched Braxton Gates's display of true friendship and I had scolded my soul for not having done more for Jonesy. I did little else but watch and pray from my bow seat, mind you. There was naught else to be done except to await our deaths and wonder who would be next. I began to wonder these things out loud and soon I could judge the minds of Gates and of Johnson. I began to wonder who's suffering would end first. I began to point about in circles to who might be tortured the longest for their sins there on the sea. They admonished me to silence such talk. They scolded me to think of fine drink and food and to await the coming coolness of night. I would not quiet. I would not obey those that I had grown to see as flawed.

I passed another hour with such talk until Braxton Gates could take no more of my mentions of our deaths. He stood upright in the stern of our skiff and threatened to come forward and toss me to the sea. He stood and threatened and Dirty Johnson found the strength to second Braxton Gates's promises if I did not quiet. That is when I chose to stand. I stood balanced behind the bow seat and I showed them my knife. I waved Jonesy's bone-handled knife from starboard to port and in a great many slow wide circles and I begged them to come forward. I begged them to speed us all to our end.

They silenced then. Johnson and Gates did not come forward and we each settled back. We each looked to the sea to face our own sufferings. Another hour of blistering heat passed before the first signs of a great storm showed itself on the horizon. The morning's red sky had indeed been a warning and we all knew what lay ahead. Each soul knew that he would certainly drown as a result of the coming storm for none of the remaining three had strength enough to weather such a building beast. Those were the thoughts that had reached my mind when I decided to look away from the coming storm. I studied instead the faces of Johnson and Gates. I did not like what I saw. I did not like the mirror of death that their faces portrayed.

They were burnt and blistered and patched with the beginning scars of starvation. Dirty Johnson and Braxton Gates were becoming shadows of men. Johnson and Gates were becoming agents of the devil while their bodies still breathed human life. They stared at me as well. Johnson was close. He was but a foot or two away and he stared not at my own signs of death but at Jonesy's bone-handled knife. I reasoned then that he was of a mind to grab up Jonesy's knife and run himself through before a more ghastly end could arise. I reasoned that he had thought himself above suffering more upon this earth and I was not about to allow him an easy exit. I took the knife from his view. I hid the knife into the back of my belt and looked again upon the sea.

"Hand over that knife, boy. I say hand over that knife," Dirty Johnson said in the low whisper of a voice he had left to him.

"I'll never. . ."

"You will boy," added Gates as he joined Johnson astride the center seat of the skiff. "You most surely will boy, or you'll be joining the others in the dark depths of the sea."

"Then we go together," I replied as I pulled the knife again from my belt and waived it in the threat of pain and of fresh blood. "You are of a mind to die easy. You both are cowards and should die hard as you have made others."

Dirty Johnson looked at Braxton Gates in a moment of awe. He had not the voice to speak his thoughts so Gates spoke for them both, "Die? Son, how in the name of the devil did you ever come to such a notion? We've a mind to live, I tell you. Do you see the coming storm, boy? Do you see what lay ahead?"

"I see a great many things. I know our deaths to be in those clouds."

"Certainly our deaths lay there boy, if we stay as we are. But we are of a mind to live."

"Live? How?"

"Hand over that knife and I'll show you. Hand over that knife and we might save you as well, boy." Braxton Gates said those words a might too bold and a might too close to my fears. I jabbed Jonesy's knife forward to meet the advance of Gates's hand and I sliced a cut upon the back of his right wrist.

He pulled back. He pulled back and thought the situation through. "You don't get it; do ya boy? We are going to die in that storm if we don't eat and eat soon. We are going to need strength to hold fast to this tiny ship."

"Eat? What fish are you going to capture with a knife?"

"Not fish boy; juicy, moist flesh," Gates replied as he pointed his blood soaked hand towards Jonesy.

I had no immediate reply. It was an awakening to realize that they were of a mind to have at Jonesy or perish. I knew inside that death awaited us in that storm; yet, I did not know which course was better? Should I die in a struggle to prevent them from carving into Jonesy's flesh? Should I hope to overpower the pair and become a killer of men? I would still die in the storm even if I could stop them. Before their advances, before their new promise of hope, I had thought I was of a mind to die. I doubted then. I hesitated in my firmness to face death like a true sailor at sea. They sensed my fear and hesitation. Johnson and Gates knew they had reached into my will to live and they again asked for Jonesy's knife.

I confess now, here on the bones of Jonesy's grave, that I was of a mind to hand them his bone-handled knife. I was of a mind to remove myself to the rear of the skiff and allow Johnson and Gates a free path to Jonesy's flesh. I was of such a mind for sure; but, what of my gold? Always the gold.

They wanted to take Jonesy's knife and start sucking some of the moisture from his flesh. Johnson and Gates desired the nourishment from Jonesy's meat in order that they might survive. I protested weakly. I protested and I protested but not, I say, with the force that I could have mustered. My protest delayed Johnson and Gates and I soon convinced my young mind that they would surely throw me into the sea. I convinced my young heart that I desired to live longer than that day. Thus convinced, I could still not bring myself to bare witness to the carving of Jonesy's flesh.

Opposite this, I did not know what our fate would be. I did not know if the three were to survive. I did not know if our little skiff would find a welcoming shore. Thus, I couldn't risk - I did not risk - I would not risk the other two finding my sixteen pieces of gold.

I could not risk them being the carvers of Jonesy's flesh and discovering my wealth. So I volunteered. I volunteered. I took Jonesy's bone-handled knife and I started to carve at the calf of his left leg. I started a deep and upward carve and Jonesy moaned. He moaned and I realized my error. I realized I had become lost in my own selfish thoughts of riches and gold. I saw then that I had forgotten that Jonesy might yet be alive. I had failed to imagine that his blob of rotting, putrid, burning flesh could still be a man. I panicked. I panicked as he moaned and wriggled under the knife and I drew it out of his calf. I drew it out of his calf and I raised it high. In my panic, I drew his bone-handled knife skywards and plunged it into Jonesy's heart. In my haste to secret a rich cache of gold, I was forced to aid Jonesy along in his struggle to meet his God. I ran that knife through Jonesy's heart and I ran it and I ran it and I ran it again. I then stabbed Jonesy six or seven times about the chest to be sure he was dead.

I was covered in the spurting and spattering of Jonesy's drying blood as I carved long slices of meat from his thighs. I carved slices and strips from his arms and I threw them to the aft section of the skiff. I made Johnson and Gates scramble for their nourishment. I made Johnson and Gates search in the blood soaked bottom of our skiff for their precious meat. I was touched with a fit of madness in those moments. I carved and I carved and I threw the meat. Parts of

Jonesy went lost to the sea. Parts of Jonesy landed on the legs and the backs of Johnson and Gates but they did not care. They stayed away from my flailing knife. They stayed back from my madness as they sucked the finality of Jonesy's mortal life.

Many a night I spend in this swamp wrapped only in a fear that my sudden and furious lust for those little bits of gold made Jonesy's last moments ever more dreadful than they would have been. I try to feel his muscle and skin being peeled away. I try to imagine my own arms and legs being thus mutilated; I cannot. I torment myself many a long and lonely night in an effort to feel Jonesy's pain. I did not cry when that knife came to its rest. I did not cry; nor did I look back upon Johnson and Gates. I felt the warm blood of Jonesy on my skin and I calmed. I let that knife fall and I calmed. I vowed not to eat of the flesh. I want that known. I want it known that I did not partake in the eating of Jonesy's flesh. I vowed to meet God's wrath for having committed the sin of murder but I would not partake in the daemon of eating Jonesy's flesh.

I looked out upon the building sea and settled into the bow to meet my fate. That storm soon blew waves twenty feet high. That storm near swamped the skiff on more than one occasion. We did have a small rudder but it was of no use to Dirty Johnson or to Braxton Gates as they continually cursed not having the ability to turn our bow into the crashing waves. The vibrating sounds of roaring, crashing waves mixed with booming claps of thunder as I held the remains of Jonesy tight against the limited safety of the bow.

I think I will talk no more of that night. If you wish to know more about that night then I'm afraid you must track down one of them other two. Talk to Johnson or Gates, if you can find them after these many years, for that night is a night that I do not choose to recall upon myself. Not that night. I rode into that storm certain that Death's horsemen would be leading my way into hell. I rode into that storm with the knowledge of the damned. There weren't no use in my praying to a God who I had shunned those moments before. I just hugged tight to the corpse of Jonesy. I pressed my face down into his exposed remains as a slight advantage against the sting of rain and waves and I could feel the roundness of the gold as my chin buried deeper into Jonesy's waist.

I awoke to the stench of my nose being pressed into Jonesy's decomposing belly. I awoke to a stillness I had not known since the twenty-eight had hoisted sail for Boston Towne. I awoke beached

28

on the shores of our colony not six miles from this black swamp through which we walk. I awoke as I had slept: alone and afraid.

I arose from the skiff to survey the scene around me. I saw two sets of footprints leading away from the skiff and I surmised that Dirty Johnson and Braxton Gates had chosen to leave me behind. They were men of the sea and they knew, as Jonesy would have known, that such a storm brings scavengers to the beaches. They knew that first light would see local folk descend upon the storm-swept beaches in search of any treasure that might be washed ashore. Dirty Johnson and Braxton Gates desired not to stand trial for their murderous ways. They desired not to stand in judgement of their having eaten the forbidden flesh. Aye, men of the sea they were and they knew of such things as scavengers after a storm.

I too was quick to learn of these things for it weren't long before the first scavengers arrived. I spied their lanterns a mile or so up the beach. They were closing in on our valuable skiff, our treasure of a beached boat. I had to leave. I had to hide from any witness to my crimes. I had a thought to run into the nearby woods while I could still go unnoticed. The trees were only a hundred yards from the skiff and I started to make for their safety; then I remembered about Jonesy and the gold. Our skiff were a fair find for the beach scavengers but not my gold. No, not my gold.

I could not pull Jonesy's dead weight from its having been wedged hard into the bow of the skiff. I pulled and pulled upon his arms and legs but to ill effect. I'll sooner drain this swamp in one brackish swallow than swear that I could have found the strength to dislodge Jonesy from that boat. I had not a thought of Jonesy's knife until then. I had no thought until that moment to cut loose my gold and leave Jonesy for the locals to find. I thought of it then. I surely thought of it then.

I did not ponder on that knife for long, I say. I could not find it in my belt nor about the boat. The scavengers were drawing ever near and my time for action appeared short. I did not think clearly at that age. When I was young, I did not reason as most men reason. I did not have the faculty of mind to think clearly from one point to the other point but, in those desperate moments, I did happen upon a solution to hiding my gold. I confess now that it was not a solution that I had reasoned from beginning to end. I had again thought of running empty-handed into the shelter of the forest that surrounds this swamp. It had been my plan to seek asylum from my crime of having killed Jonesy, the gold be damned.

My young mind reasoned that I needed to slow the discovery of Jonesy's body before I fled. My young mind reasoned that the scavengers needed to be slow to find evidence of my crimes when they discovered the discarded boat. That is why I grabbed the port side of the skiff and heaved it over onto its starboard side. I had a mind to upset the craft so that Jonesy's corpse would be hidden underneath. I had a mind to roll the boat over on top of Jonesy and run. Jonesy changed those plans as he fell from the skiff and onto the sand when the port side lifted skyward. I felt Jonesy's weight leave the boat and I allowed the port side to fall back. Jonesy and his knife were free. I had my gold.

There was no time to cut Jonesy's breaches away and escape with the gold. The locals were too close. I did not know if they had seen the boat through the rising mist of the early morning but I could not risk being discovered cutting away at Jonesy's corpse. I would not risk losing my gold either so I jabbed Jonesy's bone-handled knife into his chest and grabbed him up by the ankles. I dragged his body across the sand and into the welcoming veil of the trees. I quickly grabbed a broken branch from a nearby pine and rushed back to the skiff. I swept away all trace of my path of escape. I made it appear as if the foot prints in the sand told of but two survivors walking away from that beached and deserted craft.

I then returned to Jonesy. I returned to Jonesy's corpse and used my remaining moments of solitude to partially bury him beneath the sand and debris. I had hoped it to be enough. I had hoped in silence, as the lanterns drew nearer to the skiff, that I would not be discovered. That day passed frightfully slow. I was worn from the sea. I had not eaten a proper meal in days and I thirsted for water, any water. I hated leaving Jonesy behind. I hated leaving our gold so unguarded; but, I had to survive. After the first set of scavengers laid claim to our boat, after they had pulled it out into the surf so as to make it easier to take it to their village, I removed the bone-handled knife from Jonesy's chest and made my way deeper into the forest. I found water and nuts and a few berries fit to eat and then I rested. I did not sleep. I did not feel safe from the wild things the forest might hold. I did not feel safe from the search parties that I imagined to be hunting me and Johnson and Gates. I rested but I did not sleep.

Sleep is a thing that I have long since stopped praying for. I labor for ready cash when work is to be had in our village and then I rest. I labor hard and in silence so that I might return healthy to this swamp every night and prepare for the coming of Jonesy's soul. Sleep is a thing my body shall enjoy when the devil claims the last of the twenty-eight. Sleep is a luxury I afforded Jonesy those many years ago and I pay penance for it now. I close my eyes, to be sure, but never at my labor and never in the midst of this erie swamp. Yes, I close my eyes but I do not truly sleep.

I arose from my rest on that first day ashore to find the moon on the rise. It was not night and it was not day. I had risen from my rest in the middle ground of shadows and confusion. I had become lost to the trail which would lead me back to Jonesy. I had grown careless in my search for water and I had no notion of how to get back to my gold. I stood silent as thoughts raced around in my head. I worried that my actions had been for nothing. I worried that I had set in motion the events that led to Jonesy's death and I would have not an ounce of the gold to show for it. I worried what a young boy would do in the world, alone and unable to share his true story. I stood alone and I worried and I listened. Having nothing to say and no soul to say it to, I listened intently to the sounds of the coming night.

It was not in my mind to listen for the sea. I was lost and confused and scared; but, somehow, amidst the singing frogs and birds and crickets I heard the rolling surf as the tide came gentle onto the shore. I followed the sounds of the surf as I crashed through the darkening forest. A great many vines and branches slowed my progress but I reached the beach safely and undetected. The scavengers had gone. I could see no signs of life or lantern and I felt safe to begin searching for Jonesy. I walked north along the beach near a mile but could find no sign of where the skiff had been nor any signs in the sand of it having been dragged back into the surf. I retraced those steps to where I had exited the forest and began to walk a slow path south. The moon had yet to rise to its full height and there were but a few stars in the night sky. These things made my search for signs slow and purposeful. I could only detect changes in the sand from a few feet away.

I did not have much further to walk along that shore before the signs of the skiff would present themselves to me. I had exited the forest but a few hundred yards north from where the skiff had been; from where I had hidden Jonesy's corpse. My young heart did not know this. My young heart sank from having walked a mile or so north and then having to retrace those steps. My young heart thought of the gold and of Jonesy's bones and flesh. I saw crabs and other scavengers in my mind then. I saw a great many beasts in my mind eating upon the flesh of Jonesy and I began to cry. I began to cry the cry of a boy and I collapsed upon the sand. I had foolishly allowed myself to think. I had a young fool's heart which allowed my mind to retrace the events of the twenty-eight. I questioned and I doubted and I cried.

I was alone on the wide expanse of an uninhabited shore. I had forsaken God and I could not go home to my beloved mother and father, not after having killed Jonesy. They would know. I could never go home for I could never hide my shame from my father or mother. Be it known that I wish this solitude on no man. I had no Jonesy nor any God to console me. I had been the end of Jonesy. My actions had marked the beginning of this solitude. No, I wish this utter solitude on no man - not even Johnson nor Gates. No man should be without his God. Not Jew, nor Moor, nor Papist. No man should stand so alone.

I determined then to live out the remainder of my days never forgetting this feeling of solitude. I determined then not to live a life of joy and fullness. I had taken another man's chance at long and happy years and I would pay penance for having done this deed. I would not touch that gold, Jonesy's gold. I determined to await a sign from Jonesy's soul. I determined to await direction and guidance from the last guardian I had known. I picked my young body up from that sand and continued my search for Jonesy's corpse. I had to find Jonesy and give him a proper Christian burial. Then I could await his sign.

I found traces in the sand not far from where I had been sitting. I found the marks where the scavengers had taken possession of our skiff. It did not take me long to find Jonesy. I had thoughts of burying him there. I had thoughts of digging into the soft sand and burying Jonesy near the beach but the forest was of good timber and I foresaw the day when men would come to claim its good wood. I foresaw the day when Jonesy's bones would be unearthed and I could not allow such an occurrence. Not if I was to await his return.

I sat vigil that night over Jonesy's corpse as I have these many nights since. I sat in wait of the coming dawn so that I might find a safe and proper burial mound for Jonesy's remains. I was calm. I had cried away my fears. There was nothing left for me to understand. There was nothing left for me to question until Jonesy returned. I reasoned then, as I reason on this night, that Jonesy will return to either come to my aid or to exact his vengeance. I am prepared for either course he should choose.

That next morning I marked a trail that led me to this swamp. I knew that no one would willingly venture into this wasteland of witches and ghosts. I ventured that no amount of good timber could drive men into this swamp, even in the light of day. I had made my choice and I returned to gather Jonesy's remains. I had made certain that my path was well marked but it was by no means clear. It was a hard trail of fallen trees, wet marsh and vines. I was young and not strong enough to drag Jonesy's remains over such an expanse of waste. I resorted then to my last act of violence towards Jonesy. I acted rightly, I think. I took Jonesy's bone-handled knife and I worked hard at removing the arms and legs from his body. I acted rightly because this allowed me to carry the lighter weight of Jonesy's body to its final rest. I placed Jonesy near the spot where he now lay and I went back for his legs and then his arms. I acted rightly for certain, but I could not find his right arm upon my last return. His left arm remained where I had stacked Jonesy's limbs but his right arm had been carried off; by what beast, I do not know.

I dug a deep and proper grave for Jonesy. I even went into the nearby village and stole material to make him a burial shroud. I stole a bottle and some nails as well and, with my own urine, I made a witch bottle to place under Jonesy's corpse. I made the bottle as I had witnessed my father make his own witch bottle for under the hearth of our new home. I washed Jonesy's corpse and I wrapped the shroud around his many separate parts. I made Jonesy as whole as I could and I placed him in his grave. I then rolled his britches into a tight ball around their hidden gold and placed Jonesy's treasure by his side.

Yes, we carried the pieces of Jonesy ashore; each in our own way. Braxton Gates and Dirty Johnson carried pieces of Jonesy ashore and lost them somewhere along their escape. They scattered pieces of Jonesy through their sins and I through mine. Parts of Jonesy were left behind and I have been of a fear these many nights that his soul cannot return to an unwhole corpse. I hear now these spectral callings, these ghosts, as my friends. I see and hear these ghost in this black swamp as they set out in search of the many parts of Jonesy's temporal existence. Surely, they have gathered them by now. Surely, this is the night of Jonesy's return. He will tell me what is next to do. Jonesy will be my absolution and he will tell me through these many years what is to be done with his bones and the gold. Surely, Jonesy will know of which course and tack to take.

## ~ *The Heavy Footed Soldier*
## *or The Cookie Thief*

**Note to the reader:** *we found this in amongst my grandmother's things a few weekends ago; I can't believe she saved it. It's a note I wrote to her at a very young age . I cleaned up the grammar just a little bit ~ hope you don't mind . . .*

Gramma,

The soldiers came gramma. 'member how you promised you'd be here if the soldier's came? The soldiers came but you weren't here so I hid; I'm hiding in the cellar like you told me to if the soldiers came. I think you told me to, remember? I can hear their feet. I can hear the heavy footed one the most, specially when he opens the flour drawer. Why is he opening and shutting it so much? The flour drawer squeaks you know. No matter how slow or how fast you pull and push that rusty old thing squeaks loud and louder. Like gramps squeaks, huh! What does he want in the flour drawer? I took all the cookies.

I didn't see the soldiers too good. Just their black boots as they fell from the sky. Like in the movie ~ remember? I could see their boots coming down just above the cherry trees. I had to squinch my eyes to see through the kitchen window ~ it's kinda dirty. You should make gramps clean that window if you ever get him off the couch. So, I could barely see through the window and, oh yeah, your glass rainbow was swirling around in the sunlight ~ remember how I made that just for you in summer camp? So that was swirling around in front of the dirty window and was kinda in my way but I squinched real good. Just barely in time too. I could just see the black boots falling between the sun and your rainbow and the cherry trees.

At first I thought I'd run to call granpa. But he was asleep on the couch and you know how gramps would never wake up for nothin' so small as soldiers dropping clear out of the sky, even if they were going to capture us and everything. Serves him, I reckon. Ain't that how grandpa would say it, "I reckon"? I bet they're torturing him real good. I can't see why, what does grandpa know?

It's the heavy footed soldier again. He walks so hard it knocks dust all over my hair from the boards above me. It's almost like he knows I'm here. Like he's trying to get me in trouble by getting me all dirty before church. Maybe gramps told about the cellar. Maybe the heavy footed soldier knows my hide-out and is just playing with me. I don't think so though 'cause not even gramps knows about this place. I don't think. I'm right under the cellar steps so they couldn't see me anyway if they came down to torture me.

It's a good hiding place 'cept for the spider webs and there's no light to speak of. Gramps would say that too: "to speak of," huh. Shhh. . .

Sorry gramma it was ole heavy foot again. He's right above me. He's playing with the flour drawer. Gramps must have told about the cookies but I got the cookies. Know why? 'cause I didn't know how long the soldiers would be here. I know you said you'd protect me if they came, but you weren't here gramms, 'member how you said you'd be here. That's why I know you'd think it was smart of me to take the cookies even though I'm not supposed to play with the flour drawer. Remember how I used to make it sing? Anyway, that's how I knew you changed the cookie hiding place ever since I found your real secret hiding place in the old white stove.

Wait. Heavy foot just stopped playing with the flour drawer. Maybe his gramma hid his cookies too. I hear him now. He's looking for me, I know it. I can hear him just above the cellar door. Maybe gramps does know this place. I can't believe he told on me. He must have told, 'cause of his heart maybe. Maybe gramps is mad 'cause the soldiers came and ruined his nap. What should I do? The heavy footed soldier just stomped hard right above me. Yuk; why does dust have to be so dirty?

I have to run for it. He keeps stomping the dust like an air raid before the attack. I'll have to slip out the back cellar window like when you was looking for me to take a bath last week. I'm leaving this note by the cellar door so you'll find it gramma. I know you'll hide here too once you see that the soldier's came. Don't worry gramms, heavy foot won't get me or the cookies. Promise. A for real promise, like when I promised I wouldn't play in the cellar no more.

*Joey*

The thing about Lori is that she isn't. I shall leave you with that thought for a moment as we venture into the scenery I wish you to imagine.

Imagine a beautiful spring day full of flowers and wild grasses growing next to a perfectly painted red and white Amish barn. Do you have that image? Good; now paint yourself a slightly lighter than blue clear sky with just a smidge of pasty, puffy clouds. Are you there? Excellent.

You see, the thing about Lori is that she isn't. She isn't anywhere and she isn't anyone. This is what it has come to: the nowhere and the nothingness of a lost soul.

It wasn't always this way. There was a time when the barn was weathered and grey. There was a time when Lori was whole and it was the barn that was missing boards and beams and true color.

Lori was everyone's joy. She was light and happiness and promise. She was her mother's daughter; of this, there can be no mistake. Lori's mother? The prototype petite, perfect debutante of yesterday who invades societies with stealth and purpose. Surely you now have the images needed to move forward, so we shall. Lori's mother married the banker's son and life unravelled on schedule.

Lori came the perfect sum of years later: after the club was dominated and a husband trained. She was a bundle. Lori was a bundle of unexpected responsibility mixed with delight and Lori's mother had a plan for both. A series of nannies and well-tanned male tutors handled Lori's upbringing while Lori's mother carefully packaged her delight into small little surprises that guests could enjoy.

All was color and texture and joy. Actually, Lori's mother thought that this was her sole responsibility to her daughter. She must teach Lori color, texture and joy. Not joy from within, have you. No, though that might come, it was the joy of others that Lori's mother thought she must teach. Lori's mother would teach her Lori to read the emotions behind fake smiles and false laughter. Of course, those were Lori's mother's thoughts, not Lori's.

Lori had no time for thoughts. There were always new friends to control, fresh circles to invade. In a group Lori didn't have to be completely present - not whole. There were many cliques in her world and Lori had to somehow satisfy her insatiable need not just to be in the center of each but, instead, to become the center of each. Imagine a wagon wheel. Imagine, better, the hub of a wagon wheel. Do you see that it is hollow? That its purpose is to be a meeting place for the parts with substance? Hold, then, this image. Hold Lori softly to this new light and see her as she was that fine Saturday morning when, to her embarrassment, nature was working and not working all at once.

Lori's breasts had grown larger than she had thought possible, as she had yet to reach her thirteenth year. Nature demanded this. In one sense, this was nature working. The boys and the men noticed too, this soft flesh moving as intended. Again, nature was at work but only as designed. What was not natural, what was not intended, is how the human psyche has developed these many centuries. Thus, Lori was embarrassed as her new riding instructor focused more upon her chest than her lesson. Nature would have liked for Lori to enjoy this attention.

Lori had had a routine. Her mother had seen to that. Every Saturday, since she could remember, Lori was taken to riding lessons at the best of stables. Lori was always given a one hour lesson, allowed to practice for one additional hour and then she and her mount were given one additional hour of freedom together. One hour of freedom seldom seemed fair to Lori as this was her only unscheduled series of moments. Yet, her mother insisted that Lori be strictly carted off to tennis lessons each and every Saturday afternoon. Riding had been Lori's passion; but, tennis was another of her mother's social expectations. Tennis was to be Lori's exposure to the club and to the prying eyes of its members. Thus, then, were Lori's Saturdays all strung together into one large training ground for a life of her mother's choosing.

This particular Saturday was different. Everything was different. Ms. Sadderton, Lori's normal instructor, had suddenly moved. Lori's new instructor was young and strange and an unexpected intrusion into her protected world. His name escaped her as he announced the lesson over and Lori turned her mount away. Her time was now her own. On this particular Saturday, she did not practice as custom had dictated under Ms. Sadderton's watchful eye. Lori failed even to ride over to the large pasture, as was her routine during her third hour of riding - her hour of freedom.

Though, by then, he was well behind her, Lori still felt the new instructor's glare upon her bouncing breasts and this annoyance led her astray. His intrusion pushed Lori further and further outside the bounds of the stables' property. This had not been expressly forbidden. Not expressly. It's just that it had never occurred to Lori not to practice for one hour after her lesson; just as it had never occurred to Lori that her horse may one day wish to venture beyond the bounds of his known world. The mount accepted this new adventure with only a slight pause as Lori guided him out and onto a gravel road. Lori had often wondered where this particular road ended. It seemed to disappear into a dark thicket of woods just beyond the rise. Now she and Ranger would discover its secrets. You should know, I suppose, that Lori had named the horse Ranger.

Lori rode silently upon the road as it entered the woods and she soon forgot the instructor's stare. As the road narrowed into a trail, and the trees closed around her, Lori momentarily began to caress her new and unexplored breast with a free hand. This we shall excuse as a sub-conscious attempt to discover the strange fascination and attention they had brought into Lori's world. She only allowed a moment for this lapse in judgement. Mother would not approve, of this Lori was certain. She chose to focus instead on Ranger and the dangerously low tree branches they had begun to encounter. It was then that she first thought of turning back. Lori had planned on turning back towards the stables but the sunlight on the trail ahead held a promise of unexplored and open ground and it was open ground that Ranger sought. He wanted to run.

When Ranger broke out of the tree line, Lori instinctively knew that she was not where anyone of her stature should have been. She was on a pauper's farm. Of this, she was certain. She was surely on somebody else's working farm and those sort of laborers would surely not appreciate, nor little understand, a young woman's need to ride free through the enormous open field of blooming alfalfa

39

that her Ranger had stumbled upon.  Certainly those people couldn't appreciate that the purple grass swaying in the mid-morning breeze was a call that neither she nor her Ranger could resist.

These were Lori's thoughts at that moment and we shall leave her to them. For now, let us look again upon our barn. It is the barn of yesteryear, grey and torn. Lori will be along shortly and she mustn't see the barn red and perfect as we see it.  She must encounter the barn as it was then, the way it was at her first viewing. Quickly then we must strip away the new double doors from the front entrance and, too, the new lumber and paint.  We must weather what boards remain attached to its skeleton of beams and make them coarse to the touch. I picture that you now see the barn in this fashion and I must say that we are now ready for Lori's first arrival.

Lori first came to the barn as a turning point.  She had seen its weary shape across the large field of purple blooming alfalfa and had decided that there, at that barn, she would turn Ranger and venture back to the stables.  She hadn't planned to linger nor to hide within the barn's sickly, skeleton shape; yet, she did linger for our Lori had encountered nature again in a fashion not easily discussed. This particular call came in the form of a boy.

Lori caught a slight glimpse of a pond on the other side of the barn as Ranger prepared to turn and run once again across that lovely field.  From that perspective, Lori's sighting of the pond could have only been a slight glimpse through a few open boards and down a sloping hill.  What was not slight were the feelings shooting through Lori's body as she turned Ranger back towards the barn in a cautious walk.  She then dismounted her horse and led him slowly into the barn.  They walked across its wooden floor as Lori's stare continued to focus on the lone figure by the pond.  The barn floor was imperfect and its many holes grew less obvious as they moved away from the light of the exposed entrance.  Lori, unwilling to give up the chance of a better view, dropped Ranger's reins and continued on to the far wall.  She soon found a hiding place behind a large upright post so that she might look out at the pond undetected. A boy, a perfect boy, of about her age was fishing from the near bank of the pond and she couldn't risk him seeing her.

He wore only shreds of a pair of jeans. This, she could see. She could see also the sweet beads of sweat as they rolled down the muscles of his bare back.  Lori's eyes followed these droplets as they disappeared into the canyon of the boy's firm and refined waist. She followed too the ripples of skin and sinew as the boy cast his line effortlessly over the pond. Lori settled into her own rhythm against the rough planks of the barn wall as the fishing line was reeled and pulled back, only to be cast out again and again. She followed these moments, his movements, and noticed not the glow in his deep brown eyes as they too followed the cast of his line and the rise of the trout.

Lori also failed to notice the closeness of a house all boarded up and cold. True, there was another house to notice across the pond and further up the hill. That house was not boarded up - not abandoned. Smoke arose from that house with the warm smell of love and affection. Unheard sounds were also present but Lori did not hear the tractor nor the men across in another field as they harvested the ripe alfalfa. Lori only noticed this boy, this particular boy on this beautiful day. Ranger, for now, was content. He had wandered out into the field of swaying, ripe grass and was content.

The boy too was content. He had caught a fish earlier but it was small and had been thrown back. The boy had now snagged a large fighter of a fish and was happy that he would not have to admit defeat on this perfect day. Lori lost focus and melted even more into the boards of the barn as she moved with the graceful movements of this boy, this heaven sent young man. We shan't discuss further the thoughts of Lori for they are private and hard to relay. Know only that she was awakened by a certain moisture to her riding pants that she had yet to experience. Nature had given her this boy and the thoughts he had arisen in her felt good and perfect and she allowed herself a moment to feel the correctness of it all.

It was only a moment. She began to slowly miss Ranger's presence and she grew concerned that the boy might detect him or even her. She grew panicked at the thought that he might discover the embarrassing moisture on her light brown riding pants. She had to find Ranger. Lori knew that she must flee. Let us, however, go back to that moment when it was okay for our Lori to feel. Let us feel that moment for ourselves and for Lori. Let us remember, each in our own way, this bond nature has provided us.

Lori never rode Ranger again. We can only imagine that Lori was ill-equipped to handle the swarming of emotion and thought from the events of that day. Lori knew her mother like she knew her alphabet and she used that knowledge to never again face her new instructor's stare. This was the excuse she had given to herself then. We shall make her see, when the time is right, that her true fear was produced by having not been in control. Lori shall come to know that she couldn't continue her Saturday morning routine because, as nature intended, the lure of that gravel road would have been too strong to withstand.

The country club was her mother's sheltering domain. This is where Lori chose to hide. Lori played tennis that long ago Saturday with a fiery passion she had yet to display. Lori launched her plan of isolation with mighty serves and unstoppable backhands. It was by design, then, that Lori shocked her instructor into allowing her tennis lesson for the whole of every Saturday. It wasn't hard to have mother convinced either. Lori should, mother agreed, devote her entire energies to tennis. Though the riding stables were a fine diversion for her daughter, and allowed a mother some time to her own needs, the equestrian crowd had grown too mixed for Lori's proper upbringing. Thus, was Lori's life decided.

Her mother now took complete control of Lori's education. Lori learned, as no one before, how to surround people with happiness and joy. She learned quickly that favors appeared when people were content.

Lori learned to always smile; to always have a laugh hidden away for some right moment. Lori learned the feelings provoked by the feel of certain fabrics, even to the eye of one who cannot touch. Lori learned how colors and smells and well-placed trinkets affect the soul.

Lori learned well and, though no one could place why, everyone wanted to be surrounded by Lori. She floated on a stage untouched by the normal burdens and worries that we all share. No one could explain, without offense of course, that being surrounded by a burdenless soul was more desirable than the company of those who willingly share their sorrows. No one could explain these things because no one had bothered to think of these things. No one except, of course, Lori's mother. This was her design, her masterful plan for her Lori.

And, there were circles. Let us not forget the ever-widening circles of intermingling friends and acquaintances. Let us not soon forget that Lori had become their hub to an even greater extent than before. There were boys, to be sure, but Lori's mother advised patience in this area. "One never knows. . ." she would often say.

"One never knows, at this stage, which boy will be the greater prize."

Lori remained a presence known to all but never truly known - not even to herself. And, the years floated by. They were short years broken by balls and birthdays and finally a car. A fine new car, to denote her father's status, that promised Lori a freedom she was unsure to want. Mother was best left in control. Yes, Lori had learned well. Lori had learned by then that freedom from mother's guidance brought only embarrassment and loss.

Lori was thus surprised to find her car parked one very late and lonely night at the end of a gravel road. She had left the club early and had driven aimlessly for hours. Our Lori experienced feelings of emptiness more and more on those nights when the club scene was dead and void of interesting souls. On those nights she too became a void, a hollow hub of vapor.

I hope you have never felt as empty as Lori felt on those nights. Lori couldn't stand those rare nights when, with mother and father off in another town, her many circles would fade and vanish one by one into special outings that others thought Lori was sure to shun or be too busy to attend. Thus, have we captured Lori at the end of a gravel road; at the end of one of those nights. It was by design, I think, that Lori's circles faded on that particular night for it was destined to end with a special sunrise.

That very next sunrise was indeed special. It found Lori walking down a long forgotten path, at the end of a gravel road, with a secret anticipation of fresh dew on flowery purple grasses compelling her further forward. She thought of Ranger. She thought of low branches that were no longer a concern from the short perspective of walking. Lori held to these thoughts of Ranger as the path opened into the clearing. Lori's eyes, thus shielded by anticipation, took a moment to truly see the weeds dominating the long dry blades of uncut, unkept grasses in the once bountiful field.

Let us look beyond those weeds. Let us look ahead to what awaits our Lori. Please, look with me past the fallow fields to once again look upon our barn. It is no longer a barn of despair; it is no longer weary and worn. But, then, you would not know of this. I must remind myself of what you have yet to learn about Lori and the barn. The barn you must now see is in flux. It has been straightened, strengthened. Gone are rotten beams. Gone are warped and ripped boards. In their stead are supports and a few new bright planks. In Lori's path is a barn in the process of redemption.

Maybe, too, you are expecting a boy to be about the barn, laughing and running with fishing pole in hand. To be reading this, I might have expected him as well; however, you must now envision him not as a boy but as a man. A young man of purpose and, I suspect, angst. His pleasure was gone. This Lori could see, even from a distant tree line. There she stayed. A nights journey of lonely reflection had led our Lori to a silent path in the dark woods. Her walk down that shadowy trail of remembrance must surely have been one of anticipation. Surely, we should expect Lori to have been disappointed by her discovery of fallow fields and a changing barn. To be the reader and not the bearer of this news, I would anticipate Lori to have lingered but a minute and then to retreat back into her world of comfort and privilege.

Lori did linger a few minutes at the end of that path but she did not retreat. Lori saw, as we should see, smoke rising from a little old farmhouse. The house was slightly hidden behind a large sugar maple and a slow rise in the ground just to the left of the barn. Our brave Lori then forged her own path to that house. She worked her way around that fallow field by staying hidden just inside the tree line. Soon she was able to approach the old farmhouse out of sight of the barn and the young man. She was less than a hundred yards away from the barn when she nestled behind the corner of that old house.

One might imagine that Lori could then see the young man's rippling muscles and smooth features shine through his rough clothing. His jeans would have been old and torn as the pair he had worn years before but now they would also be stained with paints and oils and unwashed dirt. I envision his shirt to have been ill-fitting for such a young man of muscle and size. It gives my mind the appearance of having been stolen from a high school equipment room, unmissed even by its original owner.

If you see this as well, then we are now set to venture onto this new stage. We can walk about in our minds to touch and taste and smell the wonderful summer that is to surround our barn as this young man continues its resurrection. I sense, as you sense, that the beauty of young love is about to blossom. Let us blend then our imaginations as Lori retraces her steps into the hidden comforts of the wood line.

Do not worry for our Lori will return to the barn the very next morning better prepared to meet her new love. On that next day Lori wore a button-down short sleeve blouse and the perfect pair of casual shorts that her mother had insisted she wear at times when impressions should be subtle. For shoes, she chose a pair of lace up ankle-high hiking boots. With her hair pulled back and a book held loosely, Lori strode along the end of her hidden path and popped out of the wood line. She then walked confidently across that fallow field. Her direction could have suggested that her goal was the sugar maple tree. We know, however, her true goal to have been the barn. Her target was on a ladder leaned against its western wall.

Do you see him with hammer in hand and a few nails held between his lips? Do you see him not care to notice the stranger walking across the field, not care for Lori? He cares too much, I think, for the alignment of the fresh plank he is fastening. Lori sees him though. Of this, I am certain. Even today, I imagine that our Lori still sees him in this way. As yet unnoticed, Lori paced ever closer to the barn as she began to sweat with nerves of doubt. How bold her plan had seemed hours before. How light she had felt when she rummaged through her father's library to borrow a very smart looking book. Now, coming closer and closer to the sound of hammering nails, she felt heavy with anticipation and doubt.

Dialogue is to come as well. I think we need not imagine this. With a love so pure, we most surely will feel their first few words generate themselves anew. Yes, dialogue between the two will come but, for now, the young man just stares as he finally notices our Lori drawing near. In my mind, he steps down from the ladder as Lori stops moving. She becomes frozen with anticipation. He does not disappoint. I sense that the young man softened this tense moment with a gentle call. Maybe something like, "Can I help you. . ." ~ and they have begun. Their path of love has been charted.

"No, I'm fine," she replies.

"Where you going? This here's private land."

"I saw that large tree," she says as she points to the sugar maple, "I thought it would be a good place to read."

"I guess that would be alright. What ya reading?"

She did not know. Lori must have become stunned, shocked and paralysed anew. I see her rushed into a new embarrassment before thinking to just hand the book over to the young man.

"I wanted to read this myself," he suggests. "It's on my list."

"You have a list?"

"Well, not my list. I came across a list of the one hundred greatest books ever written; but, the public library only has twenty-six of them."

Lori now had her plan. Her mother, Lori's mother, had taught her well. Lori had not learned much but she had learned how to anticipate the needs of others. She could supply this need. Lori could do this and more.

The young man went on to talk about how he had turned to reading biographies. He was telling Lori about the most recent book he had read; something about Debussy's **Clair de Lune**. Lori was thinking other thoughts as he spoke, "I would like to one day listen to his music. Debussy's theory was that true music happens in the silence between the notes."

The young man expressed that he often felt this way about people. He observed that most people don't pause. That people do not think to pause and experience moments one by one. He went on to relay about having this feeling, these thoughts, when he visited a local art museum. Lori was thinking that she wanted to somehow join him on his journey of discovery. The boy had thought that the people around him were not aware that the reason they appreciate good art is because it forces them to pause and reflect. He even believed that, with practice, this was possible to do every day. Lori was amazed that a young farm boy could come up with such beliefs just from reading one book about a long-dead musical composer.

She had been searching for an excuse to return. She had wanted to find a way to invite herself back to the barn and watch the young man work. Now she had one. Lori hit upon the idea that she could invite herself back into his world with the thought that she could acquire the books that the young man could not find at the public library. I even see it as her suggestion that they read these works together. I envision and I hear through time as Lori volunteers to read out loud just as the young man begins to protest that he hadn't time to read with her, that he had to finish the barn. Yes, it was certainly Lori who had first suggested that she could read out loud while his work continued on the barn.

Clumsy introductions and details were to follow this initial, natural flow. It turns out that his name was Jeffrey. "Jeffrey Parker," he stated as he showed Lori about the barn. Jeffrey explained that the house nearest the barn had been his great-grandfather's original house. "My grandfather built the house across the pond. That's where I was born and raised," he says as he points across the pond. Lori could see no house there, just piles of rubble.

Jeffrey explained that the new owners of the land had torn down his parents' house and all of the other barns and out-buildings. Jeffrey told of how the developers had wanted to salvage the ancient barn in order to make it a centerpiece for the new housing development that would soon rise from these fields. Jeffrey told of how he was allowed to live in the old farmhouse while he worked on the barn but that it too would someday be destroyed.

Lori would later write about sensing a tear in Jeffrey's right eye as he spoke those words on their first day. Jeffrey too must have felt the stirring emotions beginning to show through his tough exterior because he broke off that conversation and quickly showed Lori into the lower part of the barn. Because of the sloping hill, the bottom floor of the barn was accessible only from the rear at a new ground level. This lower level had been long ago divided into three sections. As Jeffrey slid open the lower doors, Lori could see that the sections to her right and to her left had retained their original dirt floors but the middle section of the barn, where they stood, had a perfectly level brick floor.

The spots of sunlight showed pieces of wood splinters and shavings scattered about that brick floor and Jeffrey appeared more at ease as he picked up a wooden carving of an ancient steam engine. Jeffrey showed Lori how it had been carved out of one solid piece of wood. Even the working, turning wheels had not been added but had been carved from one solid block of scrap wood. Jeffrey then pointed towards a makeshift shelf that held eight carvings lined neatly in one row. They were of trains and of cars and of animals. "Those were my grandfather's," Jeffrey stated. "I use them as samples; one day I hope to be good enough to create my own designs."

It was with this new sense of ease that Jeffrey continued his story. He told of his father opening a letter from the bank a few years back. He told of how the letter spoke of calling in their note on the farm. His mother had cried. That is all he remembered. His father had struggled when he had first took over the operation of the farm and he had signed a mortgage to help modernize the old ways he had been taught. And now this. Now the bank wanted paid in full or they would foreclose.

Jeffrey spoke of how his father had gone to many other banks in search of relief but none would come to their aid. Jeffrey then told of how one bank held out the promise that they might help if Jeffrey's father were to get a paying job. Jeffrey would later write that that was the start of the end. His father died in an explosion at the plant only a month after beginning that new job and the local bank had possession of the farm a short thirty days later.

Jeffrey told of helping his mother through her transition. He told of a small settlement from the factory and of how he had helped his mother move to her sister's house in Kansas prior to his running away. Jeffrey could not handle being so far from his childhood home. Jeffrey could not yet let go of the memories of his father and his father before him. Jeffrey told of working in gas stations and restaurants along his route back home. He told of how it had taken him nearly a year to finally reach the farm. The house of his youth had already been torn down by the time he arrived.

He managed to get a job as a laborer with the construction firm that had been contracted to shore up the main supports of the barn. He had helped pour the new footings and place the new support posts before that phase of the job ended, before the foreman had had to let him go. The foreman explained that his company was not bidding on the final phase of finish work on the barn. Jeffrey did not waiver in his resolve to remain on the farm after hearing those words. He struck on a plan and he sought out the new owners of the land. He had thought to agree to provide free labor if the new owners supplied him with the materials to finish the barn.

At first Jeffrey's words had fallen on unsympathetic ears. One day, however, Jeffrey found himself face to face with the president of the local bank. It appears that this man was also one of the partners who now owned the land. It appears that the bank had foreclosed on the land with the foreknowledge that the partners would purchase the note from the bank. This particular man listened. This president of a bank felt compelled to listen to the power behind Jeffrey's words.

Jeffrey presented his deals and the bank president presented his counter offers until Jeffrey finally agreed to do the work for fifteen percent less than the lowest current bid. The bank president further promised that his partners would allow him to live in the remaining house while he completed the work. The partners were to set up accounts so that materials could be supplied as they were needed. Jeffrey would be allotted one hundred and fifty dollars a week on account at the local shopping mall. With this money he could buy food and other items. Jeffrey was to be given the balance of the unspent money upon the completion of the project. Thus, Jeffrey had struck his deal.

Let us now return to Lori. Imagine, as I imagine, the many fine days they must have shared together. I see them laughing and running through the fields. I picture Lori sitting against the barn and reading aloud as Jeffrey paints the boards red and white. I see lunchtime breaks where they are both leaned up against their sugar maple tree, taking turns reading to one another. I imagine long discussion about characters and plots and future plans as they swim together in the pond on the hotter afternoons.

Lori did not visit every day. In many ways, Lori remained a mystery to Jeffrey. She would always emerge from the path at the other end of his field but by no set schedule and on no pre-promised day. She left the same. Lori never stayed an entire day. Never did she arrive or depart at precisely the same time. Lori always left Jeffrey to anticipate her next arrival with suspicion. One afternoon, however, Jeffrey took control of their schedule. One afternoon Jeffrey put down his paint brush and announced that he needed to cut their afternoon short. He stated that he had to walk into town and get more supplies before the hardware store closed.

Lori did not want that particular day to end. She had wished to extend her time with Jeffrey so she volunteered to accompany him to the store. Their walk took them to the other side of the pond and past the ruins of Jeffrey's childhood home. They then walked across another fallow field of grass and weeds. This field was twice as large as the one Lori normally crossed and their conversation kept her mind occupied as they neared its edge. The woods at the other end of this field were sparse. Barely fifty yards of virgin trees remained before they opened up onto a large asphalt parking lot. Lori instantly recognized this to be the parking lot of one of her father's new shopping centers. She had been to its dedication. She had cut the ribbon. Lori began to fear that Jeffrey might find out who her father was. Lori began to fear that Jeffrey would shun her for being related to the man who, in his eyes, had stolen his land and his heritage.

Lori had always approached Jeffrey's barn from the gravel road. Lori had always entered Jeffrey's world down a long winding path through woods that seemed somehow enchanted. Lori had often envisioned Jeffrey awaiting her returns in some far away fantasy land, isolated from the cruel realities of her own modern society. Now she knew. Lori's special place was no longer an oasis at the end of the known world, unreachable but by a chosen few. In knowing the boundaries of Jeffrey's land, and its close proximity to her father's world, its charms began to melt and for the first time in her life Lori felt shame.

Lori was ashamed that her father and his partners must somehow have been involved in taking possession of Jeffrey's land. Lori had overheard her father on more than one occasion speak of that particular shopping center and of future phases of houses to be built. She could not proceed further. Lori could not bear to be seen with Jeffrey. She could not risk him finding out that her father was responsible for his losing his farm and maybe even his father. Therefore, Lori suddenly remembered an appointment and left Jeffrey at the edge of that sparse wood. She crossed back over the open fields alone. One senses too that Lori would have felt a new waive of shame as she was once again forced to step over the rubble of Jeffrey's boyhood home.

She would later write of the feelings she had had at that moment. She later wrote of how the farm and its barn had somehow lost its charm. Yet, Jeffrey's barn was still, if only temporarily, an island on which to explore the many facets of Jeffrey. For this opportunity, Lori still felt blessed. In the scraps of that same revealing letter, Lori also disclosed that she had kept at least one book from Jeffrey. In Lori's words, *she secreted it away like a wet sheet after a fitful, damp night of still trying to grow up.* Lori had secured a copy of Fitzgerald's **The Great Gatsby** and had had every intention of reading it together with Jeffrey, like they had done with so many other titles. But Lori's mother had other plans. Not for the book, mind you. No, Lori's mother had insisted that Lori join her father and mother on a week long cruise to the Carribean. Lord, how Lori had protested that trip. Her behavior seemed odd to her parents at the time. Lori had always looked forward to their little junkets across the globe. But now Lori had Jeffrey and Jeffrey would have no one.

It was thus by accident that Lori read that book alone at sea. It was no accident that reading that book made her feel empty and ashamed. Lori kept that book from Jeffrey because she felt it revealed too much of who Lori truly was. Lori felt that Jeffrey would associate Lori's family with the characters in that book and have nothing further to do with her. It was a silly notion that

Jeffrey would later dispel; but, Lori kept that book a secret none-the-less.

Their days were numbered when Lori returned. Jeffrey had finished all but one door of the barn the next time Lori walked across the field to meet him. Because of this, they had more time on those final days to relax and love one another. Lori could not have known then; but, she was to only have Jeffrey for ten more days after she returned from her vacation. She spent those days in his loving arms and I think it best that she did not know that their last parting kiss was to be the last touch of their love.

I should share with you that we have glimpsed, thus far, into this shared summer from accounts relayed to me by the many witnesses to the everyday small parts of Lori's world; these accounts are of events that Lori's mother never took time to notice. These recollections even include those of Lori's father. It is surprising to learn now that Lori never spoke of Jeffrey, not even to her friends. Jeffrey was Lori's project alone. His was a soul that she could not read. Jeffrey was a breed that Lori could not dominate with but a smile and a dash of charm.

Mostly we are able to reach back into their summer through Jeffrey's letters. I am afraid that we do not yet have possession of all of Lori's replies; therefore, for the moment, Jeffrey's letters are the slim firsthand authority we have at our disposal. One can learn a great many details from them, however, if you are patient enough to peer deeply into the blank spaces between Jeffrey's words. I hesitate somewhat to share too many of the sacred details of their private world; but, I can help you with a few glimpses. I do not think that our Lori will mind.

I do believe that Lori would have wished their summer to last an eternity. The letters we do have give a sense that she was aware of her own spiritual awakening, both in and out of Jeffrey's arms. He did not possess her in a manly way, though she had offered. He had wished to wait. Jeffrey possessed our Lori more deeply than that; Jeffrey had touched Lori's soul and had sparked it to life. Even Lori's mother noticed the change in Lori that fall. Even Lori's mother will admit to that.

The initial letter was from Jeffrey. It did not re-cap their summer; those letters came later. One might imagine that Jeffrey's first letter was a shock to Lori when she found it propped up against one of Jeffrey's carvings. It reads as follows,

*Lori,*

    *There was no time to wait for you to come around. I hate to tell you this way but I kept a secret from you because I did not know how I would do. I studied for my G.E.D. all summer and I passed. I know you don't know why I am telling you this. You must be wondering why there is a key with this letter. I am not attending my senior year of high school. I turned eighteen last week. Sorry I did not tell you about my birthday. I didn't want you spending any of your father's money on me. Yes, I know who your father is. I really didn't feel like celebrating my birthday anyway. Maybe it would have given us a reason do something memorable. Maybe next year.*

    *Have you guessed I'm gone. I joined the Army. I had wanted to wait a month or two but the recruiter insisted that I leave right away for my physical. You know, world events and everything. I will be going directly to boot camp at Fort Benning, GA. I signed up so I could be an Army Ranger. They say that I must first be in the regular infantry. They say most people don't make it out of Airborne school before they give up going to Ranger school. I say they haven't met the likes of Jeffrey Parker. The key is for a post office box. It's box number 11 at the 3rd Street post office. I paid for a year. I will write to you there. Dream of me tonight and I promise to dream of you.*

*Love,*

*Jeffrey*

*p. s. please look after my wood carvings. In case they come to do something with this place before I get a chance to come back ~ thanks.*

    Lori's reply revealed her deep-seated respect for Jeffrey. We have several early drafts of her first reply; and, in them, Lori reveals that she had been dreading the close of that summer. For the first time that she could recall, Lori had been dreading her return to her private school and her stringent social life. Lori had consoled herself only by believing that she could keep Jeffrey close in her heart. Lori wrote that she was thankful that she no longer had to worry about Jeffrey's loneliness at the farm during her upcoming, busy school year. Lori wished for Jeffrey to pursue his life as she would pursue hers. She was certain that their love would converge again in a year or maybe two.

Jeffrey next wrote a great many details about his travels and how lost everyone in basic training seemed to be. He revealed that he felt distant from most of the other recruits. Jeffrey wrote of a sense that he might have made a mistake. Jeffrey worried that maybe he should have gone out into the world and explored a little before taking such a big step. He spoke of wild stories from the many different people that he was getting to know. Jeffrey's letters state more than once that the physical part was easy for him. Jeffrey couldn't believe, however, how hard of a physical strain basic training was for most of the other boys. One of the hardest parts of army life for Jeffrey was living so close to strangers. The most difficult adjustment for Jeffrey, however, seemed to be the many rules he was forced to live by. He complained often that there were rules for eating, for sleeping, for showering, for how to fold clothes, for how and when to talk and not talk and so on. Jeffrey once wrote,

*. . . The rules around here are idiotic. I don't like being told how to do simple, stupid little things. Why can't they just tell me what needs doing and let me do it. No, I got to wait for thirty-six other swingin' richards to get in line and do everything their way ~ by the numbers. (fyi - swingin' richards is what we call each other here in B company. I'll explain later.)*

I am afraid that this excerpt does little to show how deeply Lori and Jeffrey's letter exchanges were actually fluid pieces of love and weekly updates mixing together on the page. Their letters went steadily on like this for well over six months. Jeffrey and Lori would write to each other about daily events but the letters always seem to drift effortlessly into fond memories of their special summer afternoons. Then the letters suddenly changed. In the early spring, Jeffrey became distant and somewhat consoling in his letters once he revealed that his new unit at Fort Hood was being sent to the war in Iraq. Jeffrey revealed that he was not going to be allowed to apply for Ranger school until his unit returned in a year. His letters did little to cloak his disappointment over this detail. Jeffrey's focus on not getting to go to Ranger school overshadowed, I think, his real concern. Jeffrey was dancing around his fears. He was trying to keep his fears from becoming Lori's fears. By reading this selection of the letters closely, one senses that, by not going to that special school, Jeffrey felt unprepared to go to war.

Lori must have sensed this fear because Jeffrey thanks her many times, and in many different ways, for her words of encouragement and hope. In one letter Jeffrey writes,

*Dear Lori,*

*That's a funny story you told me in your letter of April 18th. Did anyone ever find out how the guy's Mercedes ended up in the swimming pool at your parents's club? I hope they never figure out you backed into it and started it rolling downhill. I wish I could have seen your face. It would have been funny to see you chasing after a black Mercedes in a dress and high heels. Oh, thanks for the books. I find I have a lot of time to read these days. Keep 'em coming.*

*I'm afraid it took your package a little time to get to me. I am now in a staging area in the mid-east. I am not allowed to tell you where. For some reason we all have to re-write our wills and the Captain wants to see at least one personal letter to home from everybody in Charlie company. I wrote my mother and I am forcing myself to write to you. I don't know why it's so hard. I guess I can't find the words. We are different and yet so much the same. I try to not think about you and your many comforts and the boys you must meet at all those dances.*

*I want you to know that I do hold some hope that we will be together someday but you don't need to pretend if you don't feel the same way. We could change our relationship, if you want. I don't want to but if you want? I just can't face going into combat without the thought of your letters finding me. Please, let's pretend just a little longer. If that's okay? I have to cut this short. We have hot chow coming and I don't want to miss it. Might need my strength and all.*

*Love,*

*Jeff*

*p. s. The guys all call me Parker but my best friend Frank calls me Jeff. Maybe its time I grow up and drop the Jeffrey - what do you think?*

One senses that Lori grew greatly concerned for Jeffrey and her perceived role in his going off to war. Shortly after receiving this letter she finally sent him a copy of Fitzgerald's work **The Great**

**Gatsby**.  You can almost hear Jeffrey laughing on the pages of his reply as he told Lori that he did not join the army in order to prove himself to her.  Jeffrey seems to laugh at a suggestion by Lori that she was a picture perfect model of the character Daisy.  Jeffrey worried that Lori must have felt extremely shallow and empty to compare herself to such a woman.  What Jeffrey couldn't possibly understand was how deeply Lori's mother's had indeed conditioned her daughter to think and be like Daisy.  Lori's mother, as Daisy's mother before her, had trained her daughter for one event:  marrying the right, rich man.  Jeffrey included these words in his reply,

*. . . I am not Gatsby.  I am not even great.  And you, my dearest Lori, are not hollow and empty.  You are not a fake.  We are children.  We have plenty of time to grow up.  Until then, let's not worry over silly, crazy thoughts. . .*

Jeffrey's letters also provide little hints that both he and Lori continued to feed off one another in their mutual quest for growth and knowledge.  In one letter Jeffrey writes,

*. . . Thank you for sending me the book on English grammar and style.  You were right.  I find that I enjoy reading the books you send me even more so now.  It helps to truly understand the proper use of punctuation.  Now I can read them as the author intended.  Now periods and semi-colons and commas sometimes make me feel as if the author is whispering in my ear, "Okay, pause here.  Take a moment to absorb what I just wrote, what you just read".*

*My C.O. saw me reading that book and he suggested that I read Aristotle's* **Poetics***.  The captain said Aristotle would teach me how a book should be written, how a story should be composed.  Please send me a copy.  If you can find one. . .*

I envision our Lori lovingly obeying this request.  I see her in book store upon book store searching for that work by Aristotle.  Several letters later Jeffrey thanks her for the copy she sent.  He also gives us some hint of Lori's own growth during this period,

*. . . I have only just now begun to read the copy of* **Poetics** *that you sent.  I do not know which I enjoy more:  Aristotle; or, your notes in the margin.  I also like the idea you had about being precise with grammar in our letters to each other.  It makes for good practice to*

*know there is someone who cares at the other end of a sentence. By the way, congratulations on getting an A on your exam. I find it hard to believe that you have never gotten an A on a test before. Doesn't sound like the Lori I know. . .*

Lori was indeed growing. She was branching out of her world and spending less and less nights at the club. Lori's transformation was slow enough, however, to go unnoticed by either her father or her mother. She read more books and then sent them on to Jeffrey. Lori would sometimes loathe awaiting his replies. Lori sometimes felt that she would burst while waiting for Jeffrey to have a chance to read what she had already read. She hated the long waits that she had to endure before she could finally converse about what she had thought when she first read the new words and their meanings. It was around this time that Lori began volunteering at a local youth group. Thus, was Lori's state of growth when she received this letter from Jeffrey,

*Lori,*
    *Thanks for the pictures of your spring formal. You do look good in pearls. I am going to pretend that that is really your cousin in the picture with you. I really needed a new picture of you. You'll never know how much I needed fresh images and thoughts to get me up and ready for tonight. We just got our op orders from the Lt. for tonight's mission. We're finally going to stick it to them for a change.*
    *Frank died yesterday. I thought you should know that in case you wonder why I don't write about him any more. We were there for him; you should know that. I don't think he suffered too much. Anyway, I guess I am going to give his personal stuff to the Captain today. I wonder what they will do with my things if it comes to that? Send them to mom I guess. Maybe I'll ask the guys to send you back your letters. Would you want them? I shouldn't be talking like this. Don't worry.*
    *I got promoted to corporal last week. Did I tell you that? They gave me a medal for some stuff I didn't write to you about and then they put me in charge of a squad. As a corporal, I should only be in charge of a team, a squad has two teams in it, but we are short handed these days so they gave me a squad that should be led by a sergeant. That's why the guys jokingly call me Sgt. Parker now.*

*Which is okay, I guess, since no one's around to call me Jeff anymore.*

*Maybe they should get someone else to lead. Maybe then Frank would be here to kid me about writing to my rich girl back home. He used to do that you know. He used to grab my pen and say stuff like I needed more expensive ink or you wouldn't read my letters. He used to say the butler would throw my letters out with your other fan mail and stuff like that. Maybe I should write to his mom and dad. Maybe they should know how much he made me laugh. Someone should tell them that he didn't screw the pooch ~ that it was just his turn.*

*Lori, thank you for getting me this far. I don't know time anymore. I don't know today from yesterday. I just see missions and faces. Always the faces. Thanks for the picture. I needed it. Anyway, thanks.*

*J.*

He signed that last letter with but the initial J as if to signify that he was either losing his identity or that he no longer cared to recall the many images enveloping the honorable name of Jeffrey. Lori seems to have not received another letter. She wasted away that summer awaiting news from Jeffrey. News that was not to come. Her free summer months passed slow and despondent. Lori's mother was slow to notice. There were too many summer activities to notice the change in Lori's mood. Lori's father took no notice either; at least not until the mid-summer ball.

The month of June had come and gone. July was in decline as well; yet, no one seemed to notice that Lori had barely left her room since the end of May. No one noticed that she often failed to shower or dress or even eat. No one took the time to witness Lori remaining in the privacy of her room watching an endless stream of cable news channels. No one knew, or could have known, that Lori was searching for any signs of Jeffrey or his unit. All that the servants could report was that Lori often got into her car around two in the afternoon. She would always return less than a half an hour later. We can only guess that she was keeping vigil on Jeffrey's post office box. We can only guess.

Lori had not even pursued her tennis lessons once the summer had begun. Her mother was too involved with three fund-raising committees to protest or, quite frankly, to even notice. As I have stated, it was her father who first suspected that Lori was in decline.

She used to love being his escort to the mid-summer ball. This year, she declined. Her father had looked forward to this year's event. Lori's father knew that his little girl would soon be off to college. Lori's father knew that this single event would spell an end to the darling little princess he had so long cherished. Lori nearly broke her father's heart when she told him that she would not be attending the ball. Lori's father had thought to insist on her going but he had never been the father of a teenage girl. He did not feel that he had the right to press the issue.

August was an unbearable month for Lori's father. He began to ask daily questions about Lori's activities. Of course, Lori's mother had no such information. "Children move through phases," she had stated. Lori's mother believed that Lori would bubble back up to the surface when she started to plan a social schedule for her all important freshman year of college. Lori did not bubble up. Lori drew deeper and deeper into despondency and gloom. She stopped going to the post office and she stopped eating. No one really noticed her weight loss. No one ever really looked deeply enough into Lori's eyes to see her pain.

Then there was the talk of seeking professional help for Lori. Yes, there was talk of such things but Lori's mother would have no such notion cross the threshold of her house. Lori's mother would not allow such a thought to enter again into the mind of Lori's father. Their social standing would be ruined. Maybe this might have helped Lori. Maybe not. She did not share her pain with her father or her mother. Would she have shared her inner-most thoughts with a stranger? Could a stranger have really helped our Lori? With this questioning thought exposed, I suppose that I should share with you another facet of Jeffrey's correspondence.

It came in bits and pieces but Jeffrey often spoke of his dreams for his future. Jeffrey once wrote that he planned on saving his money in order to combine it with his G. I. Bill. Jeffrey was saving his money so that he might one day attend a college. He wrote of studying history and philosophy and many other useful things before turning to the practical and becoming a lawyer. Yes, our Jeffrey wished to become a lawyer. I think he would have made a fine lawyer, don't you. He once wrote of wanting to shape new laws from the stagnation of our shared history. He had thought this necessary in order to better serve society's current needs. Jeffrey aimed to be a voice, a respected voice. He aimed to listen for and then consolidate and then repeat the needs of the many underprivileged souls who had little chance of being otherwise heard. This Jeffrey intended to do; this and more. From the hot sands of the middle east, Jeffrey had expressed his wish to help strangers that he had yet to even meet.

Jeffrey had wished for Lori to join him in this journey. He had longed for Lori to wait patiently as he grew into her world. What Lori could not read, what Jeffrey could not write, was that even he knew deep down that Lori could not wait. He held this silent, unwritten thought from Lori for he wished to dream his dream a little longer. I share this with you now, this privacy of Jeffrey's thoughts that I have gleaned from his many letters, because I have chosen to think that it was with this dream of heart that Jeffrey's final moments slipped away.

I also feel that it is appropriate to share Jeffrey's private thoughts with you because they have already been discovered by Lori's father. They are no longer secret, no longer private. An important package from Iraq was sent to Lori's father. It was addressed to him at his office. This package was from Jeffrey's commanding officer and it told of how Jeffrey had been riding in a vehicle which had been destroyed by a roadside bomb. In the letter, the commander was uncertain as to Jeffrey's fate. He stated that he had been given conflicting accounts as to whether or not Jeffrey had survived the explosion. The commander stated that he believed that Jeffrey had died awaiting aid; but, he would not know for certain until the casualty reports made it back to him from the field hospital in Kuwait.

The letter went on to state that the dispensation of Jeffrey's last will and testament would have to wait for final confirmation of his death; but, too, the commander wanted to disclose that Jeffrey had left his military insurance to the care of Lori's father. Enclosed with the comander's note of condolence was this sealed letter addressed to Lori's father,

*Dear Mr. Barrett,*

*If you are reading this note then things have not gone well for me. I want to thank you for allowing me to help rebuild my great-grandfather's barn. That time of solitude allowed me to grow a little each day by being constantly reminded of my roots. I tried to make my mother the recipient of my insurance; but, she still refuses to have any part of my being here. I am honoring her request not to have, as she phrased it, blood money sent to her. Therefore, I have re-written my will and am having you named on my policy.*

*Would you please use the money to help the local library obtain some new books. Also, I left a great number of toy carvings in the lower level of the barn. I made them out of scrap wood in my free time. I was thinking maybe they could go to an elementary school or something so that the children could play with them. I think that would be better than throwing them out.*

*I know that I left town without squaring our account and saying thank you. I have to admit that I didn't really like you or your bank when I left. I have grown beyond that now. You were just doing what you thought best. I am probably owed some money for my work on the barn; please, lump it in with the insurance money.*

*Thank you,*
*Jeffrey Parker*

It had bothered Lori's father that his partners had forced Jeffrey's mother off of her land so soon after her husband's death. That is why he had given the boy a job and a home. That is why he had arranged to pay his accounts. Lori's father had been able to hold his partners' objections to this arrangement at bay only because the work was getting done. And now this. Lori's father needed in some way to reconcile this new wave of guilt. That is what led him to the barn that day. Lori's father left his office and his appointments and drove to the old barn to recover the wooden toys mentioned in Jeffrey's final letter.

Lori's father expected to find some scraps of wood and some ill made models of trains and horses. He did not expect to find a shrine to a love that had blossomed beneath his own eyes. He did not expect to find pieces of his own sweet Lori's heart scattered about the brick floor of the barn. This he did not expect.

Lori had made a retreat of the barn in which to read Jeffrey's letters. Lori once wrote that she often waited to open Jeffrey's letters until she was nestled into the lower part of the barn and surrounded by his carvings. Lori's father discovered all of Jeffrey's letters and more. Lori's father found old drafts of some of Lori's replies and he found books. Stacks of unread books were placed about the barn in piles. They had been arranged by category. Lori's father also found unused boxes and other packing material waiting to be sent to Jeffrey in Iraq. Lori's father would later relate that he had tried hard not to cry as he sat and read Jeffrey's private letters to his only child; his only daughter.

He stood and left the barn only when he could truly resolve to do as Jeffrey had willed. He stood and vowed that he would distribute the carvings and oversee the funds. Lori's father would honor this brave young man's final wish. Lori's father had a wish of his own then. His wish was to see his daughter whole again. His wish was to help Lori through her grief and to see her once again alive and brilliant with happiness. He had a plan to tell Lori gently of the news of Jeffrey's death. He was resolved to do so in order that she might begin her grief and thus move forward with her young life.

Lori's mother had thought otherwise. At first Lori's mother would not accept her husband's story. Lori's mother refused to believe that her Lori had fallen for a common farm boy. Her denial went on like this for two days and nights. Lori's father had waived the letters about several times; but, Lori's mother refused to read even a single one of their scandalous words. Lori's father then resorted to the unthinkable. Lori's father grabbed ahold of his wife and, with tears shaking down his face, he pulled her hard into the library of their large home. Lori's father threw his wife upon a leather couch and then retraced his steps to lock them both inside. He locked the door and then he read the letters out loud. Lori's father forced his wife to hear the truth of Lori's love.

Lori's father had never before stood his ground with Lori's mother. He had never been strong enough. He had never even considered not bending to her will. This was different. He was different. The events of Jeffrey's life and death had changed Lori's father and he stood his ground. He expressed guilt and remorse for the young boy and his family. He expressed shame. Lori's mother had not the power to halt those words for she did not truly understand their meaning, not yet. Lori's mother was powerless to stop her husband. Lori would be told. He insisted that Lori be told as he walked from the library and up the stairs.

Lori's mother remained. She did not follow her husband up to Lori's room. She did not rise to relieve his pain, to hold and console her husband. Lori's mother did not even think to be by her daughter's side as she was to hear the words of Jeffrey's death. Lori's mother only thought of scandal. She only thought of who might have known about this lowly mingling of Lori and a common boy. Lori's mother retraced a year's worth of memories. She recalled every hushed snicker, every hidden smile. She recalled sudden cancellations for parties and dinners. They all became the fault of this young boy. Every remembered slight became a curse from the house of Parker.

Lori did not rise or bubble up. She did not recover quickly over the course of the next few days or weeks as her father had hoped.

Lori did not care to share in her loss and, to this, her father insisted that she be allowed the space and time that she might need to regain her life. He insisted that Lori be left alone, even if that meant delaying her start of college until the spring.

She was left alone. Lori was consoled by a few servants and by her father. Lori's mother was still angry at being slighted by her husband so now she condescendingly bowed to his every wish by having nothing to do with his daughter. In her mother's eyes, Lori had brought shame onto the family name and this would not soon be forgiven. Therefore, we may lump Lori's mother in with all those outside of the family who never really noticed the slow pace of Lori's recovery. In the beginning there were days when the food that had been brought to her room would go uneaten. Then, slowly, there were days when she would rise and walk aimlessly about the grounds. Eventually, there were even days when Lori would shower and drive about town. These were the days that were noticed the least. Lori seems to have been less and less watched once she gave the appearance to be finally functioning in a normal manner.

It turns out that Lori should have been watched even closer on those days. No one took the time to note, nor can they now recall, Lori's actions as she drove about town collecting the items that she would need. No one thought to keep watch on the barn as Lori began to compile the components that she would use to build the bomb. No one ever saw the final contraption she had built along the western wall of the barn, the wall where she and Jeffrey had first spoken. Therefore, there was no one near to stop her when she finally decided to light the fuse.

They say the taking of one's own life to be a sin, to be a cause for eternal damnation. Yet, it was not truly in Lori's heart to finalize her story. We cannot believe that her plan was the destruction of her soul. We cannot allow ourselves this belief. We must believe that it was not in Lori's heart to kill all that we have come to hold dear. You must believe, as I believe, that Lori simply needed to feel. In Lori's training, Lori's mother had left little room for feelings. There was little room for emotions of any kind. Lori's training aside, her time with Jeffrey had instilled in her a deep need for love. Lori's depth of understanding was still limited. She knew only a few things well; thus, she needed desperately to experience the colors and the textures of Jeffrey's final moments. This need, not a wish of death, was most surely in Lori's heart. Her's was a burning desire to touch the final moments of a soul no longer touchable, no longer trapped. Yes, they dictate taking one's own life to be a sin but Lori shall be forgiven. Lori has been forgiven.

She did not die in the explosion. Lori's sin, that was not a sin, failed to bring about her absolute end. What did end was her well-planned existence. Colors and textures and false smiles are of little comfort to mangled hands and to eyes that can no longer see. No, Lori did not die in the explosion though it is rumored that she had. Her isolation is by choice. It is not for us to disclose her existence or non-existence at this hospital, her haven of rest. Lori will be allowed this choice and the many other choices still to be faced in her young life.

Though they say that the bandages can be removed from her eyes, Lori will not allow it. Lori will not allow light to warm the eyes which can no longer see. For now, she has chosen to hide within the cold darkness that her bandages provide. We shall allow her this, I think. We shall allow her some solitude for a few days more. Let us turn then to Jeffrey.

Lori's father visits her bedside daily. He speaks to her in kind words; yet, she does not respond. Lori has not spoken a word since the explosion, not to her mother nor to her father. Lori has chosen to continue her summer of silent vigil for Jeffrey even though she is well beyond the news of his death, well beyond the changing colors of fall. This, too, we shall allow.

Lori's father spoke on this very day of having purchased the barn and its surrounding property from his partners. Lori's father wished to discuss restoring the remaining house and converting the barn into living spaces. He spoke of wanting to reserve the new housing for returning veterans while they attend the local college. It had the sounds of a grand idea but Lori's mother wished him to not discuss such matters in Lori's presence. Lori's mother would like to have her father discuss such matters with others, maybe with Jeffrey's surviving family. Lori's mother expressed her wish that her husband would not be a daily source of reminding Lori that her Jeffrey is gone. Land and library books and other such matters might someday be decided upon; but, for now, Lori's mother needs to be allowed to finally focus upon Lori.

I myself have visited the barn and their sugar maple tree. I made sure to travel there before the sugar maple's final colorful leaves had had a chance to fall. I walked those grounds alone as I imagined Lori and Jeffrey running and laughing and falling in love. I imagined the pair reading to each other and growing inch by inch into the superior souls they were to become. My walk into Lori's wonderful summer was cut short, however, when I came across the tattered and burnt section of the barn. A hole almost two feet in diameter has been blown through some of the lower boards and the surrounding red paint is pitted and scarred black from the flash of fire and glass that took Lori's eyes.

Lori's eyes. . . they will no longer read to Jeffrey. Lori's eyes will no longer look upon their sugar maple in spring or in fall colors. Now Lori's mother reads to her daughter daily. Lori's mother has kept her vow to read out loud the many fine stories of fictional mystery and romance that Lori had purchased but had yet to read. Yes, Lori's mother strokes her young daughter's hair and reads tales of great adventures. Lori's mother may one day be bold. Lori's mother may one day begin to read to Lori about the many great people who have lived and prospered with handicaps such as blindness and crippled hands but these stories will wait. There is time enough to salvage Lori's hopes for a bright and full future.

Time is the remaining luxury that Lori's mother has allotted herself. However, I am afraid that I have taken too much yours by writing these many words. I think we have done well imagining Lori and her world. Yet, let us not leave her this final image. Let us leave the barn unscarred for her memory, for when she chooses to grow with us. Let us go back to our perfect barn of red and white and pasty, puffy clouds. Yes, Lori shall be saved in due time. As she has salvaged her mother's soul, so shall we salvage hers. So let us leave her images of Jeffrey perfect.

With these, their letters and photos and pieces of my own memories of Lori, I hope to have painted her somewhat whole for you. I wish you to know that your imagined presence here has helped. I needed the thought of you looking over my shoulder as a sort of guidance as I wrote. You may never know how much you have helped me to imagine what Lori's eyes must have seen through the years. For this, I thank you. Before I end, I want to also remember to thank you for your note of concern for Lori. It is I who should have written first. I should have consoled you on your loss of Jeffrey. You, a true mother, deserved at least that.

You are in my thoughts . . .

Love, Lori's mother

*The Good, Good Sheriff* ~

The good, good sheriff
and the bad, bad men
ran down the byway
and on past the inn.

They circled the block
three times around
like Keystone cops
or circus clowns.

I saw them run across the way
sitting safely within;
not seen by the sheriff
nor the bad, bad men.

As I wait real patient
for this comedy to play out,
I guess I could mention
just how it came about.

See I'm adrift,
no real home town;
home's a split
between lost and found.

So not long before
the events I describe
to this inn's door
I did arrive.

The first thing I see
upon arrival
is a young beauty
with no true rival;

built to withstand
years of abuse
from a redneck man
with no real truth.

So I think to myself
in a silent way:
she needs your help
to break away.

Of course, it's a challenge
I set for myself
when I go a prowlin'
new towns like an elf.

What I didn't know,
and this is the twist,
is that my little show
would cause this fit.

The town was in autumn
around election time
and the fever had caught 'em;
those voters were prime.

Well this little cutie,
that I'd set upon,
was doing her duty
from just past dawn.

She was hanging posters
of some old cuss
that set one man to bolster
and others to fuss.

Being above
such politics,
I looked for love
in my bag of tricks.

Those trade secrets
I shan't give away
but it involved sonnets
and parts from a play.

It turns that she met
my amorous advances
with her own little set
of impassioned glances.

Tit for tat
we scuttled around
and just like that
we're doing the town;

with posters that is.
These things take time
like fire from fizz
or poems that rhyme.

Like I said,
I'm real patient.
So I softly tread
with passion still latent.

The day turned
well into night
as my heart burned
for little Ms. Right.

Long story short:
nothing happened.
She had to report
to General Patton.

That's what I called him,
her father so stern,
and back at the inn
what did I learn?

Seems that the General,
who'd ended my chase,
was really the Colonel
of the posters' face.

With *Daddy* as mayor
of a little small town,
I hadn't a prayer
least I stick around.

"Do things proper,"
Inn Keeper had said,
"cause he'll sure stop her
and have you dead."

Well now, wasn't this
a cute little bind.
I should have quit
to Hollywood and Vine.

But no, I stayed ~
a challenge to defend ~
and maybe get paid
with a happy end.

Next day came
her secret note
of a hidden shame
and a secret boat.

More like a lake
than a large pond
she studied its wake
as I rowed on.

She told the tale
of her lone heart
of loves that failed
from no true start,

"daddy won't have it,
our name to defend,
so I just manage
with very few friends."

About a week
this went on:
every night to meet
at that large pond.

She asked me to ask
the Colonel a date;
no small task,
no small fate.

For now I could play
and have me some fun
but he'd make me stay
at the end of a gun.

Yet, I worked the courage
to actually speak
with a brain in storage
and two cold feet.

But before the deal
could go steadily down
words that were ill
surrounded the town.

Of how the mayor
should control his own;
that he should repair
his own loose home

before crying 'bout change
in perpetual small towns
which loosens the chains
that centuries hand down.

So, he set the sheriff
out on the prowl
for a daughter too careless
and this shady night owl.

I guess that brings us
about as far
as one day prior to the fuss,
this chase on the tar.

Note number two
came yesterday
of how she was blue
and should run away . . .

. . . with me.
*My God*
I started to plea,
*I've gotten the rod.*

Head got light
so I went about
to set things right
'till I heard her shout

at the sheriff
who was shaking her down
with the bailiff
in the middle of town.

So I did a silent mosey
back to the inn
and settled real cozy,
well-hidden within.

Day passed to night
and came note three:
I'm in a fright
*please, meet me.*

What do I do:
that which I must;
or, do I skedew
and call it a bust?

You guessed right,
for readers are smart,
so into the night
I did start.

Long story short:
we held and kissed
then began to resort
to all we had missed.

At the end of it all
we lay on the ground
watching stars fall,
not making a sound.

That's when it hit
an idea like a bolt
that when we split
I'll play a joke

on her tyrant
of a dad
from this valiant
little lad.

So I turn serious
and just happen to say,
"I'm quite curious
of the image portrayed.

"Give me details
of his life in town
of secret mails
and deals that go down."

Well she didn't know
of any such dirt
as my face did glow
with a swallowing smirk.

Facts are facts
and are often in need
of the details they lack
about incessant greed.

I've said before,
on calmer days,
and I'll say once more
to be sure it stays:

truths
not known
are not less true
once they are shown.

So I begged for names
of those in town
and the places he stayed
when out and abound.

She spoke soft,
all that she could,
as together we walked
through silent deep wood.

We parted a kiss,
on darkened street,
deciding that this
is where we'd meet

the next day
at noon.
To be on our way,
not a moment too soon.

Back at the inn
in a lighthearted mood
I picked up a pen
and wrote real smooth:

*Dear sir,*
*please let me partake*
*in causing a stir*
*from your mistake.*

*I mean no harm,*
*your daughter to love;*
*though raised on a farm,*
*I'm soft as a dove.*

*But you good man*
*have much to fear*
*for I've a plan*
*to cause you tears.*

*Time's real short*
*so I'll get to it:*
*your evil cohort*
*and you just blew it.*

*See, you messed*
*with the very wrong fellow*
*who has passed life's test*
*and won't run yellow.*

*I, of course,*
*have brotherly connections*
*with those who enforce*
*our fair elections.*

*And you, good sir,*
*are all but good*
*for the truth you blur*
*by sanctioning white hoods.*

*And the trips you take*
*at town's expense*
*all are fake*
*then and since.*

*You and that bloated,*
*bloated old sheriff*
*have too often gloated*
*over funds misspent.*

(please, reader, excuse that last line
but, hey, they can't all rhyme
'cause a pair for sheriff, no doubt,
doesn't exactly leap right out.
Yet it is a spin
about him and me
the bad, bad men
and a young beauty.
So without further delay
the letter did continue
in much detail to say
many facts about his true venue.)

*I know of lady friends*
*like Ms. Swanson*
*and the time you spend*
*at the Howard Johnson's*

*in Smithville*
*on Saturday nights*
*with your Caddy Seville*
*kept from sight.*

*The sheriff, he too,*
*is in ill deed,*
*wrapped up with you*
*in feeding your greed.*

*Cemeteries fill*
*with those who voted;*
*that they vote yet still*
*is duly noted.*

*So call the dogs off*
*your daughter and me*
*and I'll rebuff*
*my brother's duty.*

Well it went on
about this and that:
about illegal guns;
and abused little cats.

It was a joke,
I swear,
this little note
without a care.

The fictitious world,
America has lost,
in poetic word
I have brought

on this fateful day
to a one horse town;
and, who could say
the truth that it found.

The note I slipped
under the Colonel's door
at half past six,
not less nor more.

At precisely seven,
by Inn Keeper's time,
I sighted heaven
as church bells chimed.

She passed a letter
through the Keeper's hand
of how it was better
to ditch our plan.

The Colonel received
my planned little joke
and sure was peeved
by the *truth* that it spoke.

Turns out it was mostly truth
except about my brother
who's still a youth
living quiet with our mother.

"Well," she said,
"we had a good run
but he'll have you dead;
and, that's no fun.

"His job as mayor
is all that he knows
and you haven't a prayer
if it comes to blows.

"The sheriff was over
with two armed men;
you're to meet the clover
by a quarter to ten.

"Daddy is loyal
to town and career
but enjoys the spoils
that others held dear.

"This is home
to him and me;
I just can't roam
no matter the company.

"So be on your way,
my sweetness dear,
and do not delay
until you are clear."

Well how's that look,
I thought to self,
to be off the hook
and have kept my health.

The sheriff made haste
but was disadvantaged
by not knowing my face
or to where I had vanished.

The Keeper, it's true,
was in the know;
but he kept his clue,
not letting it show.

So I sat down
for one last cup
before leaving town
in my old truck.

And looking back
to a late sunrise
out there sat,
to my surprise,

two young men
across the park
sharing some gin
and nature's art.

And nature's herb,
I might add,
beyond the curb.
Isn't that sad

to see them out there
in the wide open
with souls all a bare
and having trouble coping.

I hate seeing
potential wasted:
for any *Being*
to live life untasted.

But they are young
and meant no harm;
and not all come
from disciplined farms.

So I wrote them off
as no big deal
'till the silence did stop
as lover, she squealed.

Loudly!
Loudly, from not far away,
and then stood proudly
to the sheriff as if to say

that she didn't care
for his vocation
'till she was grabbed by the armed pair
to be faced down by that old cretin.

In silent movie form, her lips then swayed
into a slow moving grin;
they seemed to say,
"he's one of them."

Well I'll be damned,
as I looked across,
if she hadn't condemned
those boys in the park.

Exposed as they were
they hadn't a clue
that my little stir,
not the herb, had caused this stew.

Long story short:
it was in the park,
that I now report,
the chase did start.

The armed pair
stood alone and dumb;
they simply stared
at a sheriff on the run.

The beauty, she waived,
a silent goodbye;
for my path was paved
under a clear blue sky

as the good, good sheriff
and the bad, bad men
ran down the biway
and on past the inn.

It's these lessons I learn,
in America's small towns,
that make my heart yearn
to spread them around.

So before I depart
this Inn Keeper's booth
I wish to impart
one very simple truth:

*all life is fiction,*
*nonfiction as well,*
*it merely depends*
*on whose weaving the tale.*

## ~ *Double Take*

Looking over my shoulder, to no avail, I assumed she hadn't noticed me. I have assumed a great many things over the years but never to this tragic of an end. (*Would you rather not know that? Would you rather not know the near-end of this tale? Would you have me share, instead, its wonderful beginning and middle? Would you, for yourself, like to decide the folly or tragedy of it all? Very well then; how is this:* Saundra was late for the type of appointment which requires promptness and grace . . . *So you like that better? Alright, I acquiesce.*)

Saundra was late for the type of appointment which requires promptness and grace. It was not set by her. It was not set for her. The appointment was not even hers to keep, but Saundra had promised her sister that she would make an appearance and play her part well. You see, her sister is a twin. Now, logically speaking, that wouldn't necessarily make Saundra a twin but it turns out that they were both twins; and, to each other.

Saundra's twin sister's name is Kelly. That is something you should know in order that you may tell the two apart. They are quite identical by every other means. It should be easy, however, for you to keep them pretty well separated being as they are but names on a page for the moment. When she walked by, I froze. I should not have; but, I did. She was . . . (*Or should I write: She is? I am never quite sure how that goes. I do believe that the phrase she was is correct in this context but such a strong use of the past tense so early in this story seems rather oxymoronic. And, by using the past tense, I do risk your making the assumption that Saundra's demise is the tragedy we spoke of earlier. I assure you that she is quite well at the moment; but, we are not talking about this moment now are we? We are talking about a fateful day and a near missed, very*

80

*important appointment and my momentary lack of any human function. So, we shall stick with the past tense.*)

She was stunning. . . (*You would think that, after all that, I could be more descriptive. But we must re-create the scene, we must remember how badly I went blank in her presence so, at that moment, flowery descriptive words would have failed me. They must, therefore, fail me now.*) She was stunning in a most uncommon way as she glowed past me like an aberration with flowing black silk for hair.

I should have been on her elevator. I should have shared that ride and we would not have this tale to speak of now. I was waiting for that very elevator. I had even pushed the button. I had actually been the one to push the button requesting an elevator just moments before she arrived. So Saundra was going to an appointment that she did not make on an elevator that she did not specifically request. It is amazing that she made it there at all under such circumstances.

It was a fine elevator. I should know because I was still frozen in front of that particular elevator a few minutes later when an overly aggressive fat man with a half-eaten, toasted bagel brushed me aside to step into it. (*Or onto it? One never really quite learns these particulars in school.*) Anyway, at this later juncture, I took a momentary glimpse inside the elevator and could see its black marble floor reflecting off of its polished walls. Had I not been still completely dazed by the thoughts of her passing beauty, I might have actually stepped on/in to that elevator at that time. As it is, I have yet to actually get onto/into that elevator - even to this very moment - because another elevator, to my rear, chimed at the very same moment that I chose to become unfrozen. I surely can report that I both stepped into and onto that elevator.

Mine was not a fine elevator at all. It was far too large for one person. Not that size matters; it's just that, right then, I had no particular need to feel any smaller than I already felt. But this is not at all why I describe that elevator in the negative. I describe it in the negative because it did not have a black marble floor and shiny reflective walls. Its floor was covered with cardboard pieced together with duct tape and its walls had what appeared to be moving blankets draped down their sides. I remember this very clearly because I was not at all made happy by my new surroundings. I had wanted to imagine that I was sharing a common experience with the young beauty who had just invaded my universe. But, she had ridden in a fine elevator and I was not.

I didn't notice the movement, not at first. We were moving, the elevator and I. It made me nauseous. I get motion sick at the slightest irregularity and something seemed very irregular about our movement. I sensed that we were going down; however, reason dictated that we most surely were going up since I needed to be on the twelfth floor to meet my brother for lunch. That was the question on my mind when the doors opened. I hadn't yet turned around from having stepped into and onto that elevator so it should have registered that I surely shouldn't have been looking at an open door. It didn't. That particular fact did not register at all.

I would like to be able to report that it didn't register because I had just then thought of a surefire method to finally perfect cold fusion but we have started off our correspondence on an honest plain so I wish not to veer off of that path now. The fact that there was even a door to the rear of the elevator did not register any more than the fact that the door to the front of the elevator was just then to my rear and quite closed. It did not register that I had in fact been going down instead of up. None of those facts registered until what I would like to refer to as the moment of *The Smell*. Not a smell - *The Smell*.

Have you eaten? I mean recently? Yes, you, the reader: have you in fact recently eaten? Only you can answer this question so please do not keep reading expecting me to answer for you. I only query (*I was hoping to use that word today*). Anyway, I only query because I strongly advise you not to read any further if you have eaten in, say, the last forty-eight hours.

*The Smell* would turn a veteran's stomach raw. I do not mean your average run-of-the-mill desk clerk kind of veteran either. No, I mean the blood and guts, maggots-taste-like-chicken kind of veteran. Had I not had the motion sickness to fall back on, I surely would have puked from the smell alone. But I had just then been presented with an excellent opportunity to record a certain type of dizzy, nauseated, double-sourced kind of puke and, not being one to miss an opportunity, I took it. Actually, I left it. I left it sloshing on the ground and spattered on the near wall of the alleyway that I had stumbled into. (*Definitely into this time. One can't really stumble onto an alleyway. Well, now that I think of it in those terms, I guess you could stumble onto an alleyway if you weren't actually looking for an alleyway, which I wasn't. So I should begin this section again so that we can end it more correctly.*)

*The Smell* would turn a veteran's stomach raw. I do not mean your average run-of-the-mill desk clerk kind of veteran either. No, I mean the blood and guts, maggots-taste-like-chicken kind of veteran. Had I not had the motion sickness to fall back on, I surely would have puked from the smell alone. But I had just then been presented with an excellent opportunity to record a certain type of dizzy, nauseated, double sourced kind of puke and, not being one to miss an opportunity, I took it. Actually, I left it. I left it sloshing on the ground and spattered on the near wall of the alleyway that I had both stumbled onto and into.

My brother works in an office building. I suppose you had guessed at that; but, did you know that his is the type of large office building that is trying very hard to be self-sustaining? By that I mean it has shops and restaurants and even public rest rooms that the average Joe can use without tugging along a key that has been chained to an old metal filing cabinet. Therefore, I often find it odd that my brother, most of his co-workers and about seventy-eight percent of the entire first fourteen floors prefer to eat across the street on the third floor of another office building.

I mention this because these had been my thoughts when I was waiting for the elevator - the one I missed. I also think it a good time to mention this because you really should know about the restaurants if you wish to fully appreciate *The Smell*. Personally, I was trying hard to focus on anything but *The Smell* at that moment. I needed to get my bearings and get out of there. I needed to not focus on the foul stench of discarded Mexican food mixing with Chinese and grease in the hot alleyway. I needed not to focus on the weeks old human feces piled in the corner, left by the homeless after their reluctant meals. Therefore, the sound was temporarily welcoming.

It was a metallic sound. Like a swinging metal door coming from right above my head. Isn't it wonderful to have been given such a distraction at the very moment I needed one? I will say, however, that the swinging metal door sound coming from right above my head was not quite as distracting as the chops of fish heads and tails landing about my feet. That, I believe you will agree, was definitely more distracting. It was so distracting that I even forgot the freshly laid layers of my own puke as I turned to re-enter what I now believe to have been the freight elevator. Its doors were closed. Its doors were closed and locked tight to anyone who did not possess the necessary security code to punch into the key pad which was conveniently fastened shoulder high on the rear brick wall of the alleyway.

Being as you are still reading, I am going to assume that you had either: not eaten in the forty-eight hours previous to reading the above section; or, you went afoul of my advise and will not eat for the next forty-eight hours. Regardless, I owe that you may need nourishment sooner or later so I have just now decided to skip ahead. I have just now had the benevolent thought of sparing you the details of how I extracted myself from that alleyway and out *onto* the busy city street. I must linger there in my thoughts, however, while I ponder a way to let you know why I needed to replace my shoes. It is not what you are thinking, I assure you. I did not then, nor have I ever, puked on my own shoes. I merely lost my shoes in the alleyway amongst the details I have just now promised to spare you.

I am now in the street . . . (*No that is not correct; right now, I am writing this story. At this juncture in the story, I am in the street. The busy city street. There, now we are on track.*) I was walking across the very busy city street wearing a pair of pleated, tan khaki pants. I wear those particular pants when I need to pull off the casual upper middle class look required to "do lunch" with my brother and his crowd of stuffed shirts and ties. I was not wearing one; you should know that. I was not wearing a tie, that is, nor a stuffed shirt. I was wearing a short sleeve button-down that was designed to be worn untucked but I have never felt comfortable with that style. Therefore, my shirt was neatly tucked into my pleated khakis as I stepped onto the opposite sidewalk with no shoes while spitting the foulness from my mouth about every third step.

Did I mention that I was no longer in the street? Did I further mention that I was on the opposite sidewalk? (*Yes, I know now that I mentioned these things. I can re-read as easily as the next person; it is just more dramatic if you believe yourself involved in correcting my absentmindedness - isn't it?*) I know one thing I am certain not to have mentioned. I have yet to mention the oddity of running directly into my brother as I looked up momentarily from my newly acquired polite spitting technique.

He was talking to her, my angel. Damn the luck of it all. My freshly married, social climbing, stuffed shirt of a brother was conversing with my little petite dark haired angel not three feet from my ever increasing embarrassment. I noticed her beginning to hand him something as I glanced briefly at her form. It was a slip of paper. I believed then, as you should now, that it contained a phone number as she tried to secret this plain white slip of paper to my brother on a public street.

She, Saundra, was dressed in some very smart business attire that did little to hide the aura of her femininity. Which is odd because, quite frankly, hiding one's femininity is the sole purpose of a woman's very smart business attire. I do not believe Saundra to be completely aware of this fact. But I was aware. In that very brief moment I was completely aware. I was aware of her shape, of her smile and of the glow in her eyes as they seemed to reflect a still image of God smiling through the clouds.

I held to this divine image as I sharply turned away ~ hoping to have not been noticed. I should have stayed turned. I should have stayed turned and I surely should have begun to walk away; but, and this is the rub, I had an incessant need. It was not a need to hold one last image of her beauty, as one might think. No, the image of her beauty was well stored in my brain and in my heart. I needed, instead, to catch some hint that this young siren had no amorous designs on my recently married brother, nor he on her. Therefore, looking over my shoulder, to no avail, I assumed she hadn't noticed me. I have assumed a great many things over the years but never to this tragic of an end.

I assumed that *they* had not noticed me is more to the point. She could have noticed me all-the-live-long-day and I could have still escaped. (*And, here is another point I wish to make: this is where I would have chosen to start the story. You voted otherwise - remember? Had I had it my way, we would be further along in this story by now and you might have already guessed at the circumstances of my eventual demise. So let us assume, then, that this is my beginning. Let us assume that we have just now begun weaving this tale for this is the part where I believe the story truly takes shape. This is the part where she speaks.*)

Patience, she speaks eventually. We will get to that. For now we need to hear my brother call out my name. Not once, have you, but several embarrassing times. Go ahead and imagine that you are in that particular situation. How do you hide in plain sight? How do you escape an insensitive relative who will make a public mockery of your every little mistake. Of course he did not know the consequences of his actions, his calling. How could he? All he knew was that I had failed to show for lunch. All he knew was that

I had failed to show for lunch (*wait I already said that - no, wrote that*). I am stuck here. I am stuck trying to help you comprehend how confused I felt in the circumstances of that moment. I was stuck then because I could not go another step away from my brother for fear that he would start chasing me down like a bloodhound in search of a freshly shot fowl. I was stuck because I could not turn and proceed back to my brother while she stood so near. Not like that. Not covered in the putrid smell of vomit, shoeless. I am stuck now because how do I make you, the reader, understand that moment. I am sure you have never been so embarrassed.

I must become as unstuck as that fateful piece of paper if we are to continue onward with this, my story. My brother did, in his fashion, start to chase me down. I hadn't moved so his was a sauntering, matter-of-factly kind of chase that he seemed to need to perform from time to time. Yes, my brother moved towards me while she remained and the paper fell.

I looked beyond my brother then. I looked beyond his awkward steps as his words became mere background noise to the motion of a flittering slip of plain white paper passing the knees of a goddess. I noticed, too, her turning heels as she slowly walked away from his sudden dismissal. I was all concentration then. I have that in me you know. I concentrated solely on a sidewalk next to a busy city street as it accepted the present of a floating white slip of precious paper. My eyes settled and unsettled as the fragile document was scraped to and fro while a thousand souls passed by my winded explanations to a brother's tireless questions.

Then I heard it. "Call me," she said. Those words spoken so softly yet loud enough to pierce the crowd still ring in my ears. All the while I remained concentrating on the little lost slip of white paper being moved here and there by careless pedestrians; let us not lose sight of that. My own questions began with a fury when Saundra had departed. I asked and asked and asked but got little or no reply. My brother gave me only basics. Her name, as he knew it, was Kelly Thompson. She had just missed a very important appointment with one of his firms senior partners - not due to her actions but due to the fact that this particular senior partner had been called away.

My brother, bless his benevolent soul, had invited her to lunch when he realized I was not going to show up. She had declined his offer. Saundra, playing the role of her twin sister Kelly, had thought it improper. Not because he was married. I am sure that my brother did not reveal that little tidbit to her. No, my angel thought it improper for her to go on a lunch date with a potential future co-worker even if it was her sister who was actually in line for the job. Sad, too, because Saundra, in the role of Saundra, seemed genuinely interested in my brother. She had followed him to the opposite side of the street trying somehow to figure a way out of her deception. I can only assume that she had decided on a phone number exchange as a last ditch effort to salvage their brief encounter. Of course we now know that I interrupted this, her final plan.

I thus forgot my embarrassment as she faded into the crowd and I slowly reached for that carefully watched after slip of white paper. My brother? Off to lunch. He drifted away saying something about shoes being required. Off to lunch; too busy to bother with such minor details as cardboard floors and swinging metal door sounds. (*Before I forget, I wish to thank you for at least listening to my details. You would think that ones only twin brother would have the time of day to sort through such matters. Oh, did I fail to mention the fact that I have an identical twin as well? Did I fail to mention that this brother of which I speak is now, and was then, my identical twin. It is quite relevant to the story. Please, do remind me to make mention of it.*)

I hatched a plan of my own in those next few seconds. I would no longer be Michael, the perpetual graduate student. I would instead become Robert, the successful lawyer. Robert, you see, is Michael's identical twin; and I, as you know, am Michael. (*There, now we have made mention of this story's most intriguing irony.*) Yes, Michael would most certainly become Robert as he, I, dialed up Kelly that very evening.

I couldn't wait for that evening to arrive. One really should wait a day or two, or maybe even a week, to place such a call. One really should follow such laws of etiquette; but, we have already established that I, Michael, have never studied law. I really should have waited at least until that evening, however. My hand contained a three inch by one inch slip of white paper with no name, no address and no limits as to when it should be dialed nor by whom. (*There, isn't that another lovely moment that we have shared. Together we have just used the word 'whom' properly - me by writing it and you by reading it. I think we deserve a cookie.*)

We have no time for cookies; heavens no. We must run to Robert's loft. I would really prefer to use the word apartment here, since that's what Robert's loft truly is. However, Robert continually corrects my usage from apartment to loft; and, since ~~we~~, I, am about to go plunder his closet, it seems only fitting that ~~we~~, I, run to Robert's loft and not to Robert's apartment. (*I am sorry reader but I really must forget you exist for a while so that I may get on with the story. Nothing personal but, as you may have noticed, it is getting rather cumbersome to tug you along.*)

While I was running, and trying desperately to not think of my lack of shoes, I had just enough time to hatch a plan to get around Jimmie. Jimmie is a pretty big guy, with a pretty big heart, but Jimmie also really appreciates Robert's really big wallet. So I needed a plan for Jimmie the doorman. I should change that description. With a moniker like that, you might think of Jimmie as Italian. Don't they all have the same middle name: *The*? Names like: Joey *The* Crusher; Frankie *The* Nose; and the like. Anyway, back to Jimmie. Jimmie the doorman was, and is, under very strict orders from Robert not to allow me into the building when he is not around. When Robert is not around that is. If Jimmie were not around he would have a very difficult time carrying out Robert's orders and I, pray tell, would have not needed a plan for Jimmie.

Indeed, I did need a plan for Jimmie at that moment but what I really, really needed were shoes. Have you ever walked alongside a road that was not meant for walking? Have you ever walked a few miles down the shoulder of a superhighway or even behind the rear of a strip mall and discovered what America discards? I have. I am so sure that you have as well that we are going to use this as a common point of reference for this very uncommon point which I am about to point out. The point is this: that very same feeling of wonderment and discovery can be attained by simply running down a busy city sidewalk with no shoes on your feet. Using this method, however, you don't actually discover discarded items; they discover you.

I was first discovered around 32nd street. I was running in that general direction near a university that I had not known to exist. Either there is a university there or there is some very large and important laboratory doing ground breaking experiments because the gum that discovered my right heel was of a type not yet known to the common man. It had a unique blend of gooey, slimy, stickiness that clung mercilessly to both my heel and to that particular section of sidewalk as we tried to part ways. Surely a graduate fellow or some very secretive scientist must have absentmindedly dropped this particular sample. There is no way on this plain earth that that piece of gum ever came out of somebody's mouth. There is no way that that particular piece of gum could be chewed, spit out or swallowed once it got into any particular somebody's mouth.

The gum was a magnificent foe; and; if this were a spy story with treasure to be secured, I am sure that it would have come in quite useful. As it was, we (*the gum and I*) finally broke free of the sidewalk a little at a time. And then again a little more. And then again a little more. . . Well this went on for about two city blocks (*which, by the way, really are just about the same dimensions as suburban blocks; it's just that they happen to be located in a city*). I left little samples of that gum about every four feet; or, about every time my right heel hit stride with the continuous running efforts of my left. I say about because I really can't report with any accuracy that some of the gum was left clinging to a new piece of sidewalk with every stride. As we have established, I am trying to be very accurate in my reporting of this tale so let us assume nothing.

The next item to discover me was on the corner of 43rd and Jefferson. This item discovered that it could very easily hitch a ride to wherever it wished to go by wedging itself between the little toe on my left foot and the toe immediately to the right of that little toe. (*I would give that next toe a specific name but I really can't recall exactly which little piggy it would be.*) It felt soggy, firm and stable all at the same time; the new discoverer, not my toe. I wanted to look and see what it was but I would have had to break stride and, as we know, I couldn't break stride because Jimmie was waiting for my plan of deception. I did try and pick at it as I ran but to no avail. It wedged itself in firmer with every rocking stride of heel to toe motion. I thought it would surely break loose as I speedily rounded the corner at 58th and Wilson - it didn't.

58th and Wilson? We must pause here. I mean we must pause there at 58th and Wilson. Why must we pause at 58th and Wilson? This is a fine question being as you are not as familiar with our fair city as the natives are apt to be. We are pausing at 58th and Wilson because that is precisely what I did. I paused and took a breath. I paused and tried desperately to wipe some of the sweat from my body. I also paused to discover that it was a soggy cigarette butt which had become wedged between my toes. Mostly, though, I paused for the hookers.

I lost my balance twice trying to pry the cigarette butt loose. It came apart as I peeled it away. Some of the paper and parts of the cotton-fiber filter remained wedged deep inside the cleft of my toes but I had no time for such trifles. I had reached my first goal: 58th and Wilson. I had reached the hookers; no, excuse me, the ladies of the street. I paused and fixed myself as best I could while I reached for my money clip to count my available funds.

I figured then that I could spare only twenty dollars for my deception of Jimmie. I had hoped it to be enough. I needed class and beauty for my plan to work and, not being familiar with the going rates, I approached a red-haired beauty to inquire. She was dressed in a blue miniskirt and a short sleeve white top that had been untucked. She had unbuttoned its bottom two buttons and had tied the lose ends of the front of her shirt into a bow about her belly button. After I finished explaining my plan, she bent over to adjust her shoe strap and, I believe, to expose the milk white folds of her breasts. She then laughed at both my plan and my twenty dollars.

Jimmie is an odd fellow. He takes his job very seriously and would do next to nothing to jeopardize his image as a very professional doorman. Jimmie is discreet with privileged information such as the comings and goings of the people who live in his building and those who visit - either by Jimmie's well-guarded front entrance or through the double locked and equally well-watched side entrance. I say that Jimmie is an odd fellow because there are certain things that will make Jimmie veer from his well practiced professionalism.

I know these things because one day last summer I really needed to invade Robert's apartment and was forced to study Jimmie and his habits for six hours while I waited for him to have to take a rest room break and leave the door unguarded. I cannot decide at this moment which I find more odd. Is it strange that an all important doorman should be allowed to take breaks and leave the building unguarded? Does not a planned absence, and an unguarded door, negate entirely the need for his existence as a doorman? Or, should I find it more odd that Jimmie can hold it for more than six hours? Neither question is relevant to our tale so we should plow ahead.

What I learned during those six hours of observation is relevant, however. It turns out that Jimmie really loves the ladies. Jimmie fancies the fairer sex even more than he loves cash tips. He loves them to death. You put a cute woman, young or old, in front of

Jimmie and his whole outlook changes. He is focused only on one thing: Jimmie. I know you might have thought that he would be focused on the lady at hand but not so. In the presence of a potential score, Jimmie becomes completely self-absorbed with the appearance of Jimmie . . .

(. . . *are you still there? Are you still with me? I only ask because I sense that you have either just taken, or really do need, a break from this story. I sense that you may need a drink or a stretch of some sort. Go ahead. I will be here upon your return. I only ask one thing: I only ask that you not blame this, your need, upon me. I really do not desire to continually harp upon this point but, if you will kindly recall, it is you who hath lengthened this tale. Had the story begun at the point of my choosing then we would have surely ended it by now. You would be upon your way and I upon mine. And, too, you certainly would not be carrying the images and sounds of a certain swinging metal door and plopping, thudding chopped-up fish heads with you to your next meal. You most assuredly would never have been exposed to the moment of* The Smell.)

So there you are and there you have it. The simplicity of my plan was to coax a beautiful, classy, but not too classy, woman to stand between Jimmie and the door of the building that contains Robert's loft. It cost me twenty dollars and thirty five cents. The thirty five cents went towards placing a phone call to a fellow graduate student named Kara. The twenty dollars went to this same Kara. Kara is a research junkie. She is a biologist by training and could be out of school by now but she keeps changing her thesis. She loves thinking of new experiments and getting them started but she finds the actual practice of recording results and reaching conclusions rather pedantic (*her word, not mine*).

The most wonderful thing about Kara, at least as it relates to the tale at hand, is that she is always in dire need of money. The second most wonderful thing about Kara, again as it relates to our story, is that she lives three blocks from the building which houses Robert's loft. The third most wonderful thing about Kara, as it relates to that particular moment in our story, is that she was home at that particular moment. And, finally, the fourth most wonderful thing about Kara is that she would have done what I asked for fifteen dollars but neither one of us had change for a twenty.

I met Kara opposite Robert's building and began immediately fielding her inquiries about my lack of shoes and the general appearance of my having just been mugged. Trifles, I kept thinking. I was focused more on Jimmie than on my own appearance. I was focused on how Jimmie would find Kara's appearance is more accurate. To that point, I was a little concerned. Kara can pull off cute - I've seen it. Kara can pull off classy - seen that too. Kara can even pull off cute and classy - I only heard about that one. So I ask you: why wasn't she pulling them off at the very moment that I needed her all, her everything? I reluctantly gave her the twenty dollars as she started to say something about owing me five when one of this story's most magic moments came. Jimmie, the all-powerful, the all-knowing, the always present Jimmie the doorman went inside to use the rest room and I was in. I ran across that street so fast that passing cars knew me as but a vortex of wind and flesh.

I didn't wait for the elevator either, if that is what you are thinking. The fact that I should have by then developed, or may very shortly develop, a phobia for elevators is not at all the reason why I didn't wait for the elevator in the lobby of Robert's building. Jimmies's brother is the reason. Jimmie's brother is the why behind my having taken the stairs, and not the elevator, in Robert's building. Jimmie's brother has a name and his name is Sam. Sam the elevator man. I have left Sam out of this particular story because it was never my plan to take the elevator in Robert's building. It was always my plan to avoid Sam the elevator man by running up the six flights of stairs to Robert's loft. And, it is still my plan to one day use Sam as a character if I ever choose to write a children's story book. One is not often presented with a character such as Sam the elevator man; therefore, I plan on reserving Sam the elevator man for future use. Besides, had I chosen to wait for Sam the elevator man and his very fine elevator then Sam the elevator man might well have informed his brother, Jimmie the doorman, that I had invaded the building contrary to Robert's orders.

Therefore, I ran. I ran and ran and ran from Sam the elevator man. (*Sorry, I couldn't resist that.*) I ran the first two of the six flights of stairs that lead to Robert's loft. I am not in good enough shape to have run all six, especially after everything I had just gone through. I even had to rest a bit on the fourth level. I do think that the vomit and the running and a certain percentage of the various moments of panic had made me dehydrated. I felt tired and weak but those last two flights needed to be climbed. I needed to reach Robert's loft in order that I might plunder his closet and use his telephone.

I needed to institute some sort of plan to phone Kelly and arrange a new meeting that very afternoon. I needed to see Kelly. I needed to talk to Kelly. I needed to possess Kelly that very instant or, I felt, my heart would burst. Yet, I had no real set plan. I had but a phone number, printed in a dainty hand, on a plain white slip of paper. I had run barefoot though the city collecting discarded items while interfacing with hookers and avoiding doormen; yet, I had not the smattering of a plan.

All would be for naught anyway if Liz wasn't home. For any plan to be effective, I needed for Liz to be home. Liz? Who is Liz, you ask? I think we can agree that every good story requires a heroine and, as our story is about to reach the good part, I thought I would introduce one now. Liz is too fine of a woman and too good of a soul for my brother. Let us establish the fact of this up front. I do hope, however, that she remains in Robert's life long enough to see him grow into the kind of man she deserves. I hope that for Liz and I pray that for Robert - she deserves such a reward and he could use the growth. Why aren't you following along? Are you stuck on some particular detail? (*What? You don't think of Liz as our heroine? Maybe you were thinking it to be Saundra? Why, because she came first? Do you even know what a heroine is. I do. I looked it up. I looked it up just moments ago because I thought we might be having this discussion. We are near the end of this story and I am trying very hard to get the details of it correctly recorded before the drugs kick in. So please, agree with me on these two things: one, every good story needs a heroine; and, two, Liz is to be ours.*)

Thank you. Liz our heroine, and Robert's new bride, was indeed home. Not only was Liz at home but she was very patient to follow me around and hear out the events of my day. Liz followed me to the kitchen where I reached into her silverware drawer and retrieved a butter knife. Liz listened as I walked to the bathroom, sat on the closed lid of the toilet and used her butter knife to pick out the remaining bits of cigarette butt from between my toes. Liz also listened while I used that very same butter knife to scrape the remaining samples of crusted over gum from my right heel.

Then Liz talked and I listened as I showered. She had a masterful idea that was to be put into motion as I dressed. While I finished my shower, Liz laid out a nice pair of Robert's dark blue dress pants, one of Robert's medium blue dress shirts and a very classy yellow tie that I dare say Robert would not have owned if Liz were not around. Liz also placed a dark pair of dress socks on the bed along side a pair of Robert's dress shoes. To complete the ensemble, Liz picked out a not too thick and not too thin black dress belt with just a hint of brass for a buckle.

I was clasping that belt closed as I walked into the living room of Robert's loft just in time to overhear Liz talking on the phone. This was not odd nor was it uncouth for me to keep listening since her conversation was part of our new plan. Liz was now pretending to be Betty, the all important lead secretary of Robert's firm. (*Hello? Are you keeping up? Okay, just so we are straight on the facts so far, let us re-cap. Liz, playing the role of Betty, is placing a call to Saundra, playing the role of Kelly, on behalf of Michael playing the role of Robert, with the hope that neither Betty, Robert nor Kelly ever find out. But at this juncture we don't know all of these facts now do we. At this juncture we think - more correctly Liz and I think - that we are calling Kelly since that is the only name we had to work with. For your own sanity on this matter of currently known names, please re-read the section about the sidewalk and the flittering white piece of paper. I, myself, must move ahead with the story.*)

Liz, as Betty, dialed the number as planned. Liz, as Betty, had then asked for Kelly as planned. Kelly's sister Saundra informed Liz, still portraying Betty, that Kelly was not home at the moment. Then Liz, as Liz, placed her hand over the mouthpiece of the phone and whispered something to me. From across the room, I whispered something in reply. As I did not hear what Liz had initially whispered, I cannot accurately report it now. I can, however, report my reply.

"What," I replied.

"She is not home" I heard Liz say as I stepped closer.

"Who is not Home?"

"Kelly."

"Then who are you talking to?"

Liz removed her hand from the mouthpiece of the phone and asked.

"Some woman named Saundra," she said as her hand slipped gracefully back over the mouthpiece.

"Roll with it," I replied.

Liz then again removed her freshly placed hand from the mouthpiece of the phone and ad-libbed the best set of little white lies I have heard in a long, long time. That dialogue shall go unreported for the moment because it is only relevant that I sum up the conversation for you. Therefore, let us not further delay the summation of Liz's phone call: *Liz, in the role of Betty, relayed to Saundra, in the role of Saundra, the importance of tracking down Kelly that very afternoon. Liz, still in the role of Betty, hinted strongly that the urgency of finding Kelly had something to do with her potential future job status with the firm - with Kelly's potential future job status, not Betty's, since Betty already has a job with the firm. Anyway, Saundra, still in the role of Saundra, told Liz, still in the role of Betty, that Kelly was in district court for the afternoon and could not be reached by phone. Saundra further disclosed that Kelly and her co-workers usually had a light meal at a certain restaurant next to the courthouse after such afternoons in district court. Liz, for the last time in the role of Betty, then politely ended the conversation by telling Saundra, who may continue in the role of Saundra for as long as it pleases her, that the firm would send a messenger to the restaurant to locate Kelly and pass along some very relevant information.*

### - End of Summary

So there we have it. Liz's new plan had to be adjusted to fit the fact that Kelly was not at the other end of a dialed phone number. Kelly was in fact due at a restaurant across town at any moment. Liz was blushing from her deceptive phone conversation and I was in a new panic. I really didn't think that I could run back across town - not even with shoes on. It turns out that I didn't have to. Liz offered to drive me. It was a fine offer and one not completely out of character for Liz. Of course there was something in it for her as well. Could you place such a call and not wonder about what kind of person would merit such attention? Could you? Liz couldn't. Liz wanted, and took, an active role in my quest for Kelly from that moment onward.

To my surprise, Liz insisted that we first stop for flowers and I found myself back inside the lobby of Robert's office building, the one desperately trying to be self-sufficient. I was under strict orders as to which type of flowers to buy and how they should be arranged while Liz waited in her double-parked car. Moments later I was whirled around by a five foot two inch tall she-devil on a mission. It turns out that Liz didn't feel particularly comfortable assigning me such an important task. I know this because she told me as much right before ordering me back out to the unwatched, still double-parked car.

I stood next to the car still wondering over the flowers. Well not over, per se, I was more wondering about the flowers. I was going to meet a woman who I had but briefly glimpsed. I was going to meet a woman with the specific intent of deceiving her by pretending to be my brother Robert. Under orders from Liz, I was to remain as Robert just, and only just, long enough to disclose the existence of Robert's wonderful wife Liz and to build up Robert's very handsome and very single brother Michael. That was it. That was her plan. It sounded simple enough except I couldn't figure out where the flowers came in; or, could come in for that matter. Why would Robert bring Kelly flowers if he were there only to briefly do all the above-mentioned things? How could Robert have a chance encounter with Kelly if he had pre-ordained their chance meeting by buying flowers for the event?

I pondered those thoughts as Liz purchased the flowers and I continued to watch the double-parked car. (*I now know the answer to those above questions. I now know a lot of answers as I jot down these details. Yes, I know also that it is killing you that I know the answers and refuse to share them now. For the purposes and flow of this story, however, I think it wise, for the moment, not to disclose all to you, the reader.*) What I should disclose now, and what I will disclose now, is Saundra's reaction to Liz's phone call. To be more accurate I am about to disclose Saundra's reaction to Betty's phone call as performed by Liz.

Saundra panicked. Saundra was rushed from her apartment by an ever growing anxiety. She was like a flood of water being forced through an ever shrinking pipe, picking up force and speed along her way. Her momentum will be building to an ever greater force as we race towards the climax of this story; so, please keep her moving steadily through your thoughts as we continue learning some other relevant facts and anecdotes that do and do not necessarily involve Saundra.

Saundra ran to flag down a yellow taxi as she worried about a great many things. Had she erred? Had she gone too far in her chasing of the Lawyer, Robert? Had she in fact jeopardized Kelly's chances with the firm of Brown, Stifland & Grey by not being early for the appointment?

You should know, too, that Saundra had done a double take of her own that morning. Saundra had purchased a bagel and some coffee and had had plenty of time to make the appointment which had not been made for her. Saundra was in fact in the correct, very large office building when a young man of about her age walked through its bagel shop and stood apart from the stuffed shirts and ties who had been vying for Saundra's attention. This young man was wearing a pair of pleated, tan khaki pants with a nicely tucked short sleeve shirt. This particular young man was reading a book.

Saundra watched this young man with interest as he sat down, read a few pages, looked up wondering why he was in a bagel shop and then promptly left. Saundra watched this young man slowly pick back up with his reading as he made his way down the busy hall off to the right of the east lobby. She followed him from a safe distance; yet, she was trying in some way, hoping in some way, to be noticed. Then he disappeared into a rest room that, Saundra was surprised to notice, needed no key. She would later recall thinking that this was indeed a very self-sustaining office building to have such fine features as bagel shops and truly public rest rooms.

Saundra would later disclose thinking those exact thoughts as she accidentally noticed the time on a very large clock mounted on the opposite wall. She was about to be late for an appointment that was really not hers to keep. It was certainly not hers to be late for. Yet, she delayed. Saundra lingered towards the near end of the east lobby until the young man wearing pleated, tan khaki pants re-entered the east lobby - still reading a book. She watched and hoped to be noticed as he gracefully finished a very interesting sentence while placing a bookmark gently into the book as it closed under the grip of his left hand. (*Don't forget to keep Saundra moving in your thoughts. Just because we are recapping her actions of the morning doesn't mean we can forget her gaining momentum towards the restaurant later in the afternoon.*)

Saundra adjusted her hair and fiddled with parts of Kelly's borrowed business attire while this young man of her desires slowly approached a large bank of elevators in the east lobby. Saundra even briefly paused right behind this particular young man so that she would be certain to share his elevator ride. She was sure to be noticed then.

The way she tells about that moment, and the way I shall now relate that moment from her perspective, Saundra felt dismissed as a nothing, as a nobody. The young man had clearly pushed the up

97

button. The young man had clearly desired to go up in an elevator but, as Saundra walked past, he just stood there. He just stood there and stared as the elevator doors sealed Saundra behind and he was gone. Saundra rode to the twelfth floor feeling as if she was not deserving. Saundra felt as if he, the pleated khaki pant wearing man of letters, had thought her unworthy of sharing even an elevator ride let alone a potential life together. Therefore, Saundra was very surprised to see this very same young man, just fifteen minutes later, wearing a suit in the waiting room of Brown, Stifland & Grey.

Enough of Saundra's very tired version of events. We left Saundra gaining momentum a short while ago and we need to rescue her before she spins out of control. Saundra was rushing to a restaurant in order to reach Kelly before our pseudo-messenger from the law firm of Brown, Stifland & Grey had a similar opportunity to locate Kelly in a restaurant next to the courthouse. Saundra needed to warn Kelly of any potential damage which may have been caused by her afternoon of flirtatious, school girl note passing. By Saundra's afternoon of flirtatious, school girl note passing. We are going to assume, for now, that Kelly remained quite professional in district court all afternoon and did not engage in any acts of flirtatious, schoolgirl note passing.

So there we have it. We have four principle characters converging on a very unsuspecting restaurant. We have Kelly who, now that I think about it, should already be at the restaurant. Oops. . .

So there we have it. We have three principal characters converging on a still very unsuspecting restaurant. (*We can still describe the restaurant as unsuspecting because Kelly doesn't know we are coming.*) We have Saundra winging across town in a rented yellow taxi. We have Liz trying desperately to drive sideways and backwards and in many other nonconventional manners in order to avoid the deplorable yellow taxis and those very rude cars which are double-parked and in her way. And then we have myself, Michael. At certain moments Michael was sitting in the front seat of Liz's car holding a very fine arrangement of red and yellow flowers. There were also sprigs of white and green in amongst the red and yellow flowers but we haven't time for such details. Michael was sitting, at times, in the front seat of Liz's car. At times, Michael was thrown out of his seat and into the passenger door by sudden and unsuspected swerves around some odd-placed obstacles. Michael was sitting, at times, in the front seat of Liz's car; at other times his head was plastered to the headliner while his rear was most definitely no longer attached to Liz's car. Michael, who gets motion sickness at the very thought of getting motion sickness, was wishing he had made the trip back across town on foot.

We must remember that, at this point in the story, none of these four principal characters are as aware as you, the reader, are about their similarities. They have not been exposed to the fact that what we are dealing with here are two sets of identical twins. You know these facts because I allowed you to know them in order that we might further the plot, as they say. For now, however, we have four principal characters who are at varying stages of awareness. Kelly knows that Saundra is her twin sister. Saundra knows that Kelly is her twin sister. Kelly does not know Michael. Kelly has yet to meet Michael and thus is very unaware that Michael has an identical twin named Robert. Inversely, Kelly has not met Robert either so she is equally unaware that Robert has an identical twin named Michael. Saundra has seen both Michael and Robert but is under the distinct impression that they are the same person. Therefore, Saundra only knows Michael as Robert and Robert as Robert even though she has seen, and became infatuated with, Michael as Michael. Michael has yet to meet Kelly but he has briefly met Saundra playing the role of Kelly. Michael knows Saundra exists because of Liz's deceptive phone conversation but has yet to put two and two and two together in order to deduce that the Saundra of the phone conversation is really the beauty who caused him to experience the moment of *The Smell*. Michael is thus unaware that Saundra is Kelly's identical twin. Liz? Well Liz is just in it for the excitement of it all. Liz is unaware of so many things that I am sure not to have enough time to detail them all here.

Liz, who at that point knew of both Kelly and Saundra, but not that they were identical twins, was very excited and pleased to have reached the restaurant before Michael got sick in her car. She had forgotten about Michael's motion sickness and felt very sorry for him as she rescued first the flowers and then Michael. Liz was very careful with the flowers and was very anxious to go inside the air-conditioned restaurant in order that they might not wilt - both the flowers and Michael. I, Michael, needed air-conditioning, a chair and a beer. I needed to settle the motion sickness. Therefore, I, Michael, agreed that the flowers should be saved as quickly as possible from the heat. Besides, I still needed to be fully briefed on the exact details of Liz's plan. My sister-in-law is very wise when it comes to romantic liaisons so I had no doubts as to her ability to lead me through the tangled mess of Kelly and Robert and Michael and, oh yes, the soon to be known, but as yet unknown, participants Saundra and Pete.

We took a seat at the bar and had a very welcoming bartender offer a pitcher of cool water for the flowers. Then the very, very welcoming bartender offered me a beer. I think he offered Liz a drink as well but my head was spinning in a web of motion sickness and anxiety and I honestly wasn't that focused on Liz at the moment. I did, however, slowly focus on the remainder of the bar area. It was tastefully decorated, as bars near courthouses tend to be. I noticed that it had two stairwells - one at either end of the bar - with brass railings leading patrons down into the main restaurant area. This, I now report, is all I noticed about the bar area before I saw the table.

It was a two person table tucked neatly behind one of the brass railings which was designed to lead patrons to a stairwell that in turn was designed to lead patrons down to the main restaurant. It was a two person table with one person sitting in its near chair. She had her back to the bar but my heart knew her to be Kelly. Yes, our Kelly. The black haired twin sister of our story.

It was time to put Liz's plan into motion. Actually, it was time for me to ask Liz exactly what her plan involved. I had hoped it involved me and Kelly and some sort of romance. Liz's plan first involved some breath mints. I had had a rough day and one never can be too safe in these matters. Secondly, Liz's plan involved my retrieving the flowers from the cool drink of water they had just received. The third step to Liz's plan involved me walking *away* from Kelly. I know; I was confused by this part as well. Liz is really a great planner of these things so have a little faith. Actually, why don't you go ahead and have a lot of faith, enough for both of us, because at this point mine was running out. Speaking of running, this would be a good time, in your thoughts, to have Saundra pay for the taxi and begin running towards the restaurant.

I still didn't understand the flowers. Well actually the flowers weren't talking so it would have been rather hard to understand them anyway. What I meant to say, and what I am now going to say, is that I still didn't understand why Liz had purchased the flowers. I remember very clearly getting up from my seat at the bar, retrieving the flowers from their water and saying, "Liz, why do I have these flowers?"

"Why? They are for me, of course."

"Of course," I replied.

And then I replied to my own reply, "Why?"

"Because Robert was a very bad boy this morning and you, as Robert, have bought them for me. You, silly, are meeting me here and those are my flowers"

"Of course," I again replied but with more force and understanding.

I then jotted down a mental note that I would really like to retrieve now but I can't. It seemed rather important at the time. It must have been rather important because I am not the kind to go around jotting down much of anything, let alone mental notes. I fear that I may never retrieve that particular stored away, once important piece of trivia so we might as well continue to describe Liz's plan. Actually, how about a little summary:

*I was to approach Kelly with Liz's flowers and re-introduce myself as Robert. I was then somehow to get Kelly to join both Liz and I for dinner so that we could all come to an agreement that Michael is the cat's meow. And, I was to do all of this by going down the stairwell at the opposite end of the bar from Kelly, cutting through the restaurant and then approaching Kelly as I ascended the stairwell that she was sitting next to. That, in a nutshell, was Liz's plan.*

~ End of *this* Summary

Would you like to know what really happened? Me too. I would love to tell you, from my perspective, what happened next. I can't. They tell me that my memory loss is from the effects of the concussion. I remember Liz sending me on my way and that is all. However, I have interviewed several of the witnesses. I even interviewed them separately so that we could have an accurate account of each of their perspectives. I even took notes during their respective interviews.

From Pete's perspective. Oh, that's right you don't know about Pete. Pete is involved through a slight error on my part because I broke a very basic barroom rule. I broke several very basic barroom rules to be more exact. These rules were thus: you never, ever approach a lady sitting at a table alone in a bar unless you have observed her for at least fifteen minutes; and, you never, ever approach a lady sitting alone at a table in a bar if there is an unattended drink at her table. These rules exist for a reason. If you wait the required fifteen minutes of rule number one then you can be pretty well-assured that the lady isn't waiting for someone special. If you can't be assured of that, then you can be assured that she is tired of waiting for someone not so special. Either way you are safe to approach. The second rule, the rule about the drink, is self-explanatory. Unfortunately, I broke that rule. I didn't see Pete's unattended drink because, quite frankly, I didn't look for Pete's unattended drink.

This doesn't really tell you a whole lot about Pete, however. Pete is Kelly's husband. Pete is also a lawyer. Pete had met Kelly for drinks to celebrate. Kelly had successfully saved a senior partner's butt after it was discovered that he was going to miss a very important hearing. "It was all last minute, you see." Those are Kelly's words, not mine. Pete had a pretty good perspective of my fall because Pete was sitting with his back half turned to the brass railing of the stairwell as I ascended to what I thought was going to be a pre-planned, chance encounter with Kelly. Only Kelly. Of course I should have suspected that Kelly was married. Women of her beauty are rarely single and alone. Wait. I should be honest here. I didn't at all suspect Kelly to be married. As I knew it then, she had attempted to hand my brother her phone number. She had had intentions for Robert that very morning. According to Pete, I initially looked beyond him and right at Kelly. I was holding tightly to the flowers and I was climbing the last few stairs and I was definitely focused on his wife. That is according to Pete. Also according to Pete, I suddenly stopped.

We can only assume that I stopped because I finally noticed Pete. Liz's plan, my plan and, I dare say, even God's plan for me and Kelly didn't in the slightest way involve Pete. I must have regained my composure because, again according to Pete, I started to put my foot on the very top stair when Saundra rushed up the stairs and breezed past me in a panic. Pete didn't specifically see Saundra trip me, not specifically. Pete did have a good enough perspective to be able to look down the stairs and see my head smash against the bottom step as my right wrist twisted behind my back. Pete did witness that.

Kelly's perspective is slightly different. Kelly was focused on the flowers. Kelly had the best of all perspectives of the moments which led up to my fall but she chose instead to focus on the flowers. To Kelly's credit she had no idea, as you had no idea, as Pete had no idea and as I had no idea that the moment Kelly decided to focus on the flowers was but a few precise moments prior to when I either fell or was tripped or was made to fall down the stairs by some otherwise undetermined means. That we shall credit to Kelly. According to Kelly's statement, she, Kelly, first noticed the flowers and then the sharply dressed young man carrying the flowers. Kelly then looked away from the young man and the flowers and began to scan the room which contains the bar and other assorted objects. Again, according to Kelly's written affidavit, Kelly states, and I quote Kelly, "I was looking around the bar area trying to guess at who the flowers might be for; therefore, I did not directly witness the exact events which caused Michael to fall down the stairs."

Liz's perspective is only slightly different from Kelly's because Liz was sitting further away from, and behind, Kelly. Liz, as we have determined, was sitting at the actual bar in the bar area. I state now that Liz's perspective was only slightly different from Kelly's because Liz, too, was focused on the flowers. Liz did, however, notice quite a few more of the moments which led up to the moment of my fall than Kelly wishes to admit to having witnessed. Liz had one very distinct advantage over Kelly. That advantage was the simple fact that Liz already knew that the flowers were for her. For Liz - not Kelly. More precisely Liz already knew that the flowers were for Liz. (*There, I have now fulfilled my promise to Liz to make sure that everyone who is anyone understands that the flowers were in fact meant for her, Liz.*) Therefore, Liz did report in her verbal, non-written, statement that she did in fact concur with the fact that the flowers did in fact pause for a brief second just prior to the moment when they would have reached the top of the stairs. Liz also stated that she did in fact witness a young woman, that she now knows as, and believes to be, Saundra, skirt past Michael at a high rate of speed as the flowers once again decided to ascend the remaining stair. The conclusion of Liz's perspective has, by her own admission, become slightly tainted by the fact that Liz has gotten to know, and really quite likes, the above-mentioned Saundra. Therefore, Liz's official version of the exact moment of Michael's fall is to be recorded as follows: "Michael fell because he was slightly bumped by Saundra and lost his grip on Liz's flowers. In an valiant effort to save Liz's flowers, Michael lost his footing and fell."

Saundra would like to go on record with the following statement: "I, Saundra, being one of the parties in question, would prefer not to go on record with a statement at this time."

And what about Robert? I really do hate leaving Robert out of most everything but, being as he wasn't at the restaurant, his perspective of the events which led to the moment of my fall really are quite irrelevant. Actually, Robert's perspective is quite irrelevant to anyone's understanding of most of the events of this ever-lengthening day which now finds me semi-conscious and with a newly throbbing head. I think that the initial round of pain killers is beginning to wane. (*Yes, wane. You really must begin to trust me in these matters.*)

When we all arrived at the hospital separately and/but together, we had quite a good time of it. We really were laughing and enjoying a very detailed recap of the day's events. There was a whole lot of "Who's who?" and, "Oh, I see!" statements being bantered about, even by the doctors and nurses. But, then two very distinct occurrences occurred that were to lead to the downfall of our very jocular mood. The first occurrence was the hospital insisting quite sternly on being paid. After we laughed a little longer, the hospital softened to a request of at least the promise of someday being paid. Then, after the hospital staff really got to become acquainted with Liz, they began asking for at least some assurance, at a minimum, that the cost of the drugs could somehow be guaranteed. The second above-mentioned occurrence, which was to lead to a further dampening of our spirits, was a very unreasonable demand made by my brother Robert and, surprisingly, Kelly the wonder lawyer.

I dare say that the pain in my right wrist began to dissipate just about the time I was writing about my brief sidewalk encounter with Saundra and Robert; therefore, I really can't contest any negative opinions that you might have about this story, at least beyond that juncture. I must allow that the drugs had taken affect at or about that point.

Had I known that it would have taken Robert so long to secure me a hospital room, I surely would have asked for more drugs. You see, I have no health insurance and, though the doctor really wants me to stay and observe - I mean stay for observation. Shall we try again? Although the doctor really would like for me to stay a day or two for observation, administration thinks otherwise. The hospital administration had wanted to not treat me at all. This particular administration, at this particular hospital, thought it best to have me transported across town to the county hospital. However. . . (*this is a pretty big and important however; so, please try and focus just a little while longer. Thank you.*) However, this particular hospital's administration was unaware, until a few moments ago, that the patient in emergency room bed number three had been accompanied to emergency room bed number three by no less than four - count them four - lawyers: Pete; Saundra; Kelly; and, of course, Robert.

Which brings me, I suppose, to the point of my writing. Are you wondering, as I am wondering, why, in my state of disrepair, am I bothering to write the details of my day in such detail? I am currently in a hospital. I was recently transported to this hospital via a very loud but well-mannered ambulance. (*Liz let them know about my tendency towards motion sickness.*) Anyway, I was put in that very well-behaved ambulance upon the request of three lawyers and one very concerned sister-in-law.

Yes, I am sedated and lying prostrate in the emergency room bed that they have chosen to number as the number three. I am writing on very strict orders from two of the four above-mentioned lawyers. This is in fact the very unreasonable demand that I mentioned just four paragraphs ago; therefore, you should be left with little wonder as to why our once jocular moods have turned sour. At least mine has turned sour. I have as yet thought to get a report on the matter from the other players in our little drama. Can you believe that one of the lawyers even insisted that I jot down *everything* that I can recall. "Spare no detail," she had insisted. Therefore, I decided many, many pages ago to give those two lawyers exactly what they had requested. A very fine nurse fetched me some paper and a pen; and, Liz, bless her heart, was dear enough to purchase a dictionary from the hospital gift shop. It is a crossword puzzle dictionary but has, none-the-less, proven quite useful; wouldn't you agree?

As for the two of the four lawyers who demanded that I keep writing through the pain, I hope that they are just now eating. I hope beyond hope that they have decided to visit the hospital cafeteria so that they will be well prepared to read about the moment of *The Smell*. I have a broken wrist for crimanie sakes! "Write all of the details down while they are fresh," he had exclaimed. Okay Robert, then you try and keep that hospital jello down. I wish now to say to any other readers - besides you Robert - that I am sorry. I mean rather that I am sorry, reader, about the last few paragraphs. I had to vent. My wrist is beginning to hurt again. I had better end this story soon.

Oh, did I mention that I am now in a semi-private room? Yes, yes and it is a very spacious room at that. I do believe that it will become even more spacious once they have all gone. I guess that I could not have mentioned my new room to you since they took my pen and paper, and even my new crossword puzzle dictionary, while they were moving me upstairs to the twelfth floor. We rode in an elevator. That should please you. Saundra and I finally rode in an elevator together and we even made it to the twelfth floor together. Everyone was on the elevator. Everyone except for Robert. Robert probably won't appear for at least another twenty minutes. That should allow me just enough time to sum up this summary for the two lawyers in question.

I would like to sum up for Robert and Kelly that I fell. That is it. That is my summary. My fall was an accident which was, and still is, no particular person's fault.

Oh, you could blame Saundra a~priori. Yes, you could blame Saundra in an a~priori way. Did not her actions earlier in the day lead to her state of panic and hurry? However, If we can use an a~priori argument to build a case against Saundra then we most certainly could build a similar case against Michael. But, I, Michael, as we know, am the victim of the fall. So let's move on.

We could, in fact sue the taxi company. How dare they get Saundra to the restaurant at precisely the time necessary to have her bump or even, I dare say, trip Michael? Surely it was Saundra's taxi driver's fault for having either driven too fast or too slow. No? Okay then, let us move still further on.

Maybe we should sue the bartender for having the courtesy of putting Liz's flowers in some nice cool water. Did not the bartender's actions make the flowers harder to grip in Michael's moment of lapsed concentration?

Maybe we could sue the elevator company that designed the elevators in the east lobby of Robert's building. Had they had the foresight to install some sort of tractor-beam to pull me into my initially requested elevator then Saundra, as Kelly, and I, as Michael, might have met in that particular elevator and the remaining above-mentioned events which led to my fall would not have occurred.

Should I continue? I could you know. I am going to allow something, I think. I am going to allow you Robert, and you Kelly, to borrow my new dictionary so that you might together look up the word **ABSURD**! I fell. I fell due to one and only one set of faultless circumstances: Life. Now may we please move ahead to the recovery aspect of this tale? My wrist hurts.

Oh, there's Robert now. I think I shall keep writing. I shall play the part of a reporter for you. Now won't that be fun? I shall continue to write and every once in a great while I shall look up and feign interest in Robert's words. Yes, I do believe that would be fun. Let us try.

Robert has just now stated that his appearance is to be brief. Robert would like to point out that Robert has several very brief points to make. First, Robert would like to point out the fact that Michael really should get a job. Second, if Michael were in fact to have a job then his subsequent lack of health insurance would not be an issue. And third, oh here we go. Thirdly, Robert would like to demand that Michael never again repeat his afternoon of plunderous behavior. His plunderous behavior towards Robert's closet and Robert's clothes. (*There, now, that should clear up one of your lingering questions. See how it is all coming together? I have had an internal running bet with myself that you were wondering why, so many pages ago, I had chosen the word plunder for my planned actions towards Robert's closet. Now you know. I certainly could have used the word pillage. Pillage would have been a perfectly acceptable word in that and, I am sure, in many other situations. But, by using the word pillage, how could I revisit my behavior if some moralistic piece of conscious thought should dictate? Pillage - er - ous? I dare say you would have stopped reading. I dare to say this because I do believe I would have stopped writing at the very moment such a word escaped my pen.*)

Robert has precisely nine suits that, he believes, must stay in their precise rotation in order that a different suit would be worn on any given Tuesday. If the rotation is properly kept, again according to Robert, then this Tuesday's suit will be different from last Tuesday's suit and, I dare say, from next Tuesday's suit.

Of course this system also works for Wednesdays and Thursdays and so forth. Yes, Robert's lovely nine suit rotation system works rather well for Robert. Just don't try and point out to Robert the very fact that a six suit rotation would net similar results. For that matter, so would a five suit rotation and even an eleven suit rotation. One could even go as far as suggesting a thirty-six suit rotation. Just don't make such a suggestion to Robert. Unless, of course, he has been drinking; but, that is quite a new and different story now isn't it. Let it be said that Robert was just now more than a little miffed that my plunderous behavior has brought a sudden and drastic end to his current nine suit rotation.

Personally, I think that Liz and I should conspire to buy Robert a new suit on every suitable occasion. I do say that Robert might well faint at the thought. You should know that I am no longer actively reporting Robert's exact words or behavior. I suppose that you should know this because Robert left a few moments ago. Actually, they have all gone.

They have all just left. Kelly with her husband, my brother with his suit and Saundra with my number and a promised tango once my wounds heal. They all have just now left and I am glad for it. My night nurse is a goddess who appears to be neither married nor a twin. Liz? You inquire about poor old forgotten Liz? Well now, Liz is lingering behind to help me. Liz thinks it very important that I not muddle my initial interaction with the night nurse. I told you she was the heroine.

*Love in Three Acts ~*

Imagination plays in act one of some fairy tale and I'm alone walking an ancient forest trail. I cross stage left to upper-right as the lighting man changes day to night; slowly, ever so slowly. In the aftermath glow of this, the opening scene, I'm center stage next to a rippling stream. It flows over the floods and into the pit, downstage center to slightly left.

Then I remember my cue, as a leaf floats by, and I look up for you to catch my eye. Behind the flowing dress of ancient days are perfect breasts concealed; yet, there, my eyes can't stay. Curling around, stare reluctant to leave a chest to ruffled sleeve, I see elbows folded around a basket of flowers and confection and I look up to meet glaring eyes and a face of perfection. I hold this, my upward stare, as the curtain falls on me and you ~ the love struck pair.

Then the fantasy cranks up as houselights dim ~ ~ act two. We're riding a ship on stormy seas, being chased by some evil sent to imprison you or murder me. Protection 'tis now my goal and I lose sight of perfection while passions grow cold. Macho muscles flex, and heart goes black, as I bark out orders to those who can't bark back.

I notice not as your frail stance changes, seemingly unamused by the apparent dangers. But you, oh you turn back a glance as blocking directs you down stage left. Your strong voice soon finds a solo to the crowd, "Can I love," you wonder, "a man so proud . . ."

Then you bend over a ship's rail rocking to the thunder of special effect, ". . . for won't it lead to years of neglect?" A teardrop signals the end of your speech as you toss back flowers to a forgotten beach.

Before I know it, it's act three where I deliver you up to a father's safety. The king, it is said, is joyed by a safe return while your prince to marry promises me employ *'till the fires of hell no longer burn.* By his side at all times, with you so near, it's me who'd then shed a tear.

I'm written too proud, and fairly bold, to live life trapped in a jealous cage. Being thus enlightened, I stare downward as lights once again fade onto a blackened stage. So I cross to the apron, as a spot makes me blind, to stop on my mark and feel a curtain seal you behind.

Opening my mouth to deliver the point of this tale, eyes tear up and skin goes pale. The audience awaits the gist of my fate: am I hero, villain or spy on the take? I sink away from this, the blinding spot, from an audience awaiting a hero, a villain or a spy novel plot. I just stand and quiver and forget my part, dreading the cold shivers of a broken heart.

When somewhere hidden from behind the light, I feel a palm's caress and a kiss to restore my sight. Paradoxically, I sense, parts are reversed as you deliver an ad-lib line ever so unrehearsed: you wonder, what's the dream that's made me cry as you bend to kiss my other eye.

*Jeffrey ~*

There you are sleeping, book folded about your chest. Do, please, know that I am here. Through miracle of miracles see me in your dreams. See us together as I do. See us running and laughing through life ~ through fields of flowers under a warming sun. Please then, dream us in a pause. Dream us with cool mountains as backstage props to hide the gods from our folly. I shall join you there.

Dream as I have dreamed these many weeks. Subtle, soft hopes that my legs were still with me; that I were still whole. Imagine me a man and not the wheelchair I have witnessed you notice. It was not my war. It was not your war; yet, you are my sacrifice and I desire to be yours. Are you a maiden of sorts? Are you a nanny just released from her duties? Or maybe a schoolteacher, fresh from giving life to our youth? Why do you sweep into view everyday at this hour? Why have the late afternoons become my folly?

I cherish these days. I cherish the days when your reading is interrupted by a peaceful nap. I do not imagine you tired and worn. I imagine you content and at rest. When you sleep, I can imagine a great many things. When you sleep I can look upon your beauty without fear of discovery and you, if you choose, can look upon me as whole.

Yes, dream the dreams that I would dare if the gods would but allow me your type of restful slumber. Dream the dreams that shall take us to faraway lands of exotic extremes. I wish that I had a spyglass. I desire strongly to know what you were reading. Do we share the same interest? I find mine have changed since my days of youth and vigor. Oh, listen to me. Have I aged a century in the last year? Have I grown so far distant from the boy I was? Was I as bold as some would recall; or, was I but a tool of war?

I read of gods now. Not the eternal God of the Jew or the Gentile. No, I prefer to read of the lesser type of gods that one can be assured were invented by man. The gods created by philosophers and poets and men of mystical mystery. I prefer to peer into these other souls in their quest for truth and understanding. I once foolishly sought such truth in fiction. I did not know it then, but my soul had once yearned for growth beyond farms and animals and the lesser sort of human interaction. I believed all authors to be great men and women of letters, the keepers of truth and knowledge. Few, if any, can satisfy that thirst in me now. I do admit that certain authors transcend mere fiction and come close to touching my soul. I choose not to call their works fiction. I choose to believe that they knew at the time of their writing that they were creating beyond the popular culture of the day. Yes, certain authors of fiction I will allow.

Are you frightened? Why do you fidget so? I have often wondered, these many days, why a tree to sit against? Why not a bench? Are you afraid of sharing, of being invaded by unwanted approaches that a bench seat would invite on your behalf? I do not know if it is your beauty which reminds me or the way that large oak is supporting you now. But I am reminded. I am reminded of a young and beautiful girl with whom I would sit in a similar posture as we would read to each other for hours. Ours was not an oak. Our special tree was a sugar maple which stood alone in an open field of hay.

I am glad this is one of your reading days. I enjoy watching you flip the pages at a rapid pace. I enjoy knowing that you are being entertained by your reading. I enjoy equally the moments when you pause. You do have a rather sincere look of reflection at those moments. I imagine you growing then. I imagine you in a university tower being enlightened and chosen. Chosen? Yes, I have begun to use my words carefully; and, I think it rare in this world to witness the growth of a soul. Few are chosen to have the ability to look beyond the scope of their environment. Few are chosen to be able to reflect wisely. I imagine you thus, when you pause. I had hoped to be one of your kind. It is not to be so.

I would like to look beyond my anger and pain. I fear that these daemons have captured me. You experience pain as well. I know. On the days that you write and read the letters, you often have a look that suggests that defiance and angst are in a struggle for your heart. But somehow you grow beyond your moments of pain and sorrow. You return to your tree in peace. Who are the letters from? To whom do you write and wait expectantly for replies?

I must confess that your actions of last Tuesday disturbed me to a point where I almost wheeled myself away. The doctors forbid this. They do not want me to operate this chair; but, on that day, I nearly needed to be defiant. It was hard to witness you almost in tears, ripping apart the envelope and letter you had been reading as you walked up the path. What did you write in your response? You tore at that paper like a whirlwind of anger and desire. I counted over ten pages as they flew carelessly to your side and you began instantly to fill another. Who causes you this pain? Who is so important to warrant such replies?

I had intentions of writing letters of my own today. I usually read while I wait the afternoons away for your arrival; but, lately, I have grown tired of reading. I find my strength weakening and to read sometimes a struggle. This afternoon I requested pen and paper. I thought it time to finally address my mother. I have not been able to post a letter to her since the time of my injuries. I have not known what to say. I still do not know how to pierce the barrier I created when I went off to war so soon after my father's death. I want to write to her but I do not know how to quiet her protest in my memories long enough to expose her to the horrors she predicted.

And, what of Lori? My dear sweet Lori. I have freely chosen not to write to her for these many months though I had much to share. Once the fighting grew more and more fierce, and friends began to leave me to struggle on without them, I saw little need of furthering Lori's pain. I had no right to hold fast to such a beauty of youth and promise. In my hardened state, I had no right. She is a fine girl with a bright future. I am sure she needs little comfort from me nor my words. But my mother? I could not write to her today; maybe tomorrow.

Will you be here tomorrow? It is a Saturday. Do you visit your tree on Saturdays? I had wanted to find out last week but there was no one to wheel me here. Will you dream for me again tomorrow? Where will we go? Asia or maybe Europe? Fine dreams they would be. A finer dream would be for you not to sleep. A finer dream would be for you to remain awake and to come close and hold my mangled hand. A much finer dream that would surely be. For today, let us dream together. I grow weary from writing.

Where are you now? Have you reached our meadow? Have you painted the mountain backdrop the gods have requested? You haven't moved for quite some time. I will assume you have paused. I will assume you are waiting for me to give up this pen and paper and drift towards you. If only I could. If only I could allow my head to fall in the warmth of this perfect afternoon. If only ~ ~ ~

Post script:

*Dear Mrs. Parker:*

*We found this piece of writing in Jeffery's lap on the day that he finally succumbed to his wounds. I apologize that it was not included with his other effects; I selfishly desired to hold onto his images a few more days.*

*You should know that, in Jeffery's final days, his favorite activity was being wheeled to a nearby park and being left there, on his insistence, for most of the late afternoon. We now know why. From our previous correspondence, you already knew that we held little hope of Jeffery's complete recovery; however, I am sure that his passing has come as much of a shock to you as it was to me and my staff.*

*I enclose this last piece of Jeffery's writing not only for your keeping but also to allow you the inner-peace of knowing that he must have finally found the restful slumber he so desired. For myself, I choose to believe that Jeffery's last moment was spent joining his fair maiden in her dreams. Out of respect, we have not tried to identify this particular young lady.*

*With all our prayers,*

*William H. Kelly*
Director of Patient Services

## Peter, Paul and John ~

Dearest Martha,

Not much going on tonight. Ted took care of the inventory and ordering again. He keeps doing that before I get a chance to get to it. Oh well, gave me a chance to play nine holes and come home early. That reminds me, Peter sends his love. Says we might get the first cruise ship of the season in a few weeks. It would be a bit early for one to put in don't you think? We could sure use it. It's been a hard winter on a lot of businesses around here. This town really needs those tourist dollars - maybe too much. Well, good night Martha ~ love you.

March 3rd

Martha,

Guess who came home today Martha? That's right, your kid is back. Came into the restaurant all cocky and arrogant like he already owns the place. I know it's barely the first of March. I know he should be in school. I must confess that I wasn't surprised to see him but I would have thought he'd come to me with his head down. Instead, he just started to lie again. Lies poured out of his mouth as soon as he walked through the door. I asked him what he was doing home and do you know what he told me? He told me that he had taken his midterm exams early. That's what he told me.

Changed his story real quick when I went behind the counter and got out the letter from last week. I haven't told you about that letter. I was secretly hoping it wasn't true. I guess it is. Maybe waiving that letter around would have had more effect if it was still crisp and official looking? When I first read what it had to say I got so mad that I threw it out. Ted had dumped a load of coffee grinds in the garbage can before I had sense enough to fish the damn thing back out. So there I was waiving this brown stained piece of paper back and forth but boy you should have seen Tim's face turn white when I told him what that rag of a letter had to say. I think I yelled something to the effect of, "It's real funny that a university of this stature would allow someone to take midterm exams when they had already kicked him out of school!" He sure as hell didn't have anything to say to that. I tell you Martha your kid can sure piss me off. He just left me standing there waiving that stupid, brown turd looking letter around. I think the customers were more embarrassed than I was. I tell you what though, I could barely steady my hand to cook after that. I suppose it was about 11:30 when I finally gave up even trying. Nothing went right today Martha. Not even when I tried to leave. The damn rear screen door got stuck again. I almost put my foot through it trying to get outside.

When I finally got to my truck something else happened that I really can't explain. I just felt so hollow. I started to shake harder. Then I just went empty. I managed to get as far as putting the key in the ignition but I couldn't turn it. I wanted to but I couldn't. I know that my mind was still inside my head but I had an erie feeling like my thoughts were floating in some strange new kind of free space. I just sat there watching the past week float by. I had really thought I could handle Tim coming home the way you would have. I really did want to be nurturing and all that. I even had all these great planned out conversations. There really is a part of me that understands that Tim has got problems and that he might need my help. I really did want to be there for him. But what did I do? I screwed it all up. Every thought I had over the past week went right out the window when he began to lie to me again.

It was near one o'clock before I felt well enough to drive home. I was scared too, I tell you. I know that much. I didn't know what I might be driving into when I pulled into our lane. I was praying both that Tim would and would not be home. I was glad that he wasn't but now I sort of wish he had been. I don't think I'm going to get much sleep tonight thinking about what I might say when I see him again. It's 12:35 now Martha. I don't figure he's coming home tonight. Maybe tomorrow. Well good night dear ~ I love you.

116

Dear Martha,

I got to the restaurant late today. Do you remember that we have the Chamber breakfast the first Thursday of every month? Of course you do. How silly of me to forget that you're the one who always had to remind me. Well I got to work a little late and 'you know who' was there. He had an apron on and was slinging fried eggs around like he'd been born to it, like he was settling into a new life. I really wasn't prepared to see that. Maybe I was still a little shaken up over yesterday. I know I really should have stayed to talk to Tim but it really hit me hard to see him behind that counter. We didn't waste all that money and effort to see him end up like that did we? Well I didn't! I don't think anyone even saw me that's how fast I walked out of there. I went down to the golf course and had an early lunch with Peter.

Not much else to report. I had a good talk with Peter. I really think that now I can handle a good sit down with Tim. I sure do wish you were here for this. Diapers and 2 a.m. feedings were nothing compared to this. I am going to stay up a little longer in case he comes home tonight. He might not. I think he might be seeing that girl again. I heard she broke it off with the Johnson boy a few weeks ago. I know Martha. I know. You always did like that girl but I think she's bad for the boy and we're not getting into that again.

Let's not end this note like this. Let's not. I'll write a little more later - after he comes home . . .

. . . sorry about that Martha. I fell asleep last night before I could say I love you. I'm going to work now. I'll give you an update on your Timothy later - if there is one.

I'm back Martha. It's a little after seven and I am going to take a quick shower but what a day. Tim came into the restaurant around 7:30 this morning but I was way too busy to have it out with him. He just put on an apron like he was going to go to work so I let him. I guess I didn't know what to say without yelling again but everything seemed to be going okay until Ted came in around noon. I tell you if it isn't one thing it's another. Ted came in the back door ready for work, took one look at Tim and quit. Just quit on me.

*Told me flat out that he wouldn't work for us another day if Timothy was going to be around. I had to drive all over town looking for him. By the time I found Ted he was half drunk at the V.F.W. hall. Got me half drunk too before I could talk him into coming back. Let me take a shower and I'll tell you how I did it . . .*

*. . . that felt good. So here's how I talked Ted into staying. I promised him that Timothy would be gone in two weeks. That's right Martha, two weeks. I don't care how you feel about it. You know me and promises. I have never willingly broken one and I won't start now. All I have to do is figure out how to get Timothy on the right path in less than two weeks. Ted's future is in that restaurant. He's worked for us since he was thirteen years old. He was even kind enough to remember to write to us that two years he was in the Marine Corps. Do you remember how proud that made us feel? Well I do. We owe Ted a future Martha. No, Timothy can't take over the place. We've had that talk a thousand times. He needs to find his own life. Like I did. Like you did. I love you Martha but I'm standing firm on this one. I think I hear the door. I'll write more later . . .*

*. . . well I guess it's good night Martha. Tim didn't have it in him to open up to me tonight. Maybe tomorrow. I think I am going to force a conversation tomorrow. I think I have that right - it's my money that just went down the drain by his getting kicked out of school. I know. I know. Keep my cool. I'll try Martha. Good night ~ I love you.*

*March 6th*

*Well Martha I had my little talk with junior today and get this - he doesn't need an education. That's right it turned into that old song and dance. "Well father, you never went to college . . ." Said he could just as easily make money off the tourists like me and everyone else in town. Crap. I wish he'd stop throwing that in my face.*

*So what did I do? Yes Martha, you know me too well. I wish I could keep my composure at moments like that but I can't. I just can't. I took that kid all the way back. I mean way back. I logged all the stuff we gave him: toys; trips; the whole works. And then, yes, I brought up the D. U. I. again. Well, apparently, he needs to hear about it again. That's what got him kicked off the basketball team isn't it? In my opinion that's what got him so far off track with his whole life.*

*Remember how you and I argued about what to do? I remember you cried a lot. You always did cry a lot. Why? We had a good life. Didn't we? I remember you really fought me about what to do about that D.U.I. but I won that one. Do you remember how much our insurance rates went up?*

*I know you think I took away his senior year by making him work but he needed it. Besides that was his choice. As I recall, we gave him a choice to either get a job and pay for the insurance or I would sell his damn car. Fought me too until one day he saw one of his friends test driving his Mustang. What was that boy's name? You know, Ray and Cindy's boy? Tim got really bent out of shape when he saw that kid spin the tires as he drove that car away from the house. That Mustang was nothing but a blue streak by the time Tim figured out what was going on. Went to work the next day as I recall.*

*Maybe if we had the D. U. I. laws they got now? Well maybe they'd have taken his license. Oh well. What's done is done. I hate that he keeps throwing my lack of education in my face. Don't I already have enough reasons to feel inadequate? You know I always planned on going to school. You know that right? I got that construction job down in Virginia when I first got out of the Army and I thought I'd ease into night school but the next thing you know I'm a foreman. Then came my first marriage and then the divorce. Well, we don't need to talk about those things. But damn it. I did okay. I got through those times okay. And then a few more years went by and I was doing well enough to even take a vacation. Imagine that - a whole entire vacation - and me with no education and all!*

*I don't know why I'm repeating all this to you but I sure let Tim finally hear the whole story of how we met. It was that vacation ~ remember? You'd come out from Iowa to sell your art on the boardwalk and I'd come to do some hiking and some soul-searching? Never got around to the soul-searching part, did I. I remember you all pert with that little bob haircut you used to wear. Well, Tim got the whole story of how we "decided" to fall in love and how then we couldn't decide between Virginia and Iowa so we just stayed right here.*

*I don't know Martha. Maybe I am the wrong guy to give Tim advice. He keeps throwing my mistakes back in my face like they're universal . . .*

. . . I'm back Martha.  I was just now thinking that maybe Tim should spend some time with Peter.  That would do him some good.  Actually, a hell of a lot of good.  A few hours with Peter is bound to set anyone on the right path in life.  I should give Pete a call in the morning and see if I can't set something up.  Well good night Martha.  Thanks for listening ~ I love you.

*March 7th*

Dearest Martha,

Well today didn't exactly go as planned.  I got ahold of Peter this morning and he said he would really like to spend some time at the beach if Tim would be kind enough to drive him out to the point.  Tim fought me on that one.  He actually called Peter "The Freak in The Wheelchair."  I didn't know people looked at Peter that way.  He has cerebral palsy for Christ sake.  What is Peter supposed to do about that?

I don't know what I was hoping might happen.  You know Peter.  Something positive could have happened, right?  It was a good idea wasn't it?  I was really disappointed when I asked Tim how their day went.  He just told me that nothing happened and kept on getting ready for whatever he was planning on doing tonight.  I had to prod him into telling me that "nothing" really meant that he had wheeled Peter to the edge of the lookout and that Peter had just sat there.  I asked him what they talked about and Tim said they didn't talk about anything.  He said that Peter just stared out at the ocean.  I had to tell your boy that Peter wasn't just looking at the ocean - that he was playing golf!  Your kid just gave me an empty look when he heard that, like my words had just created a big void behind his eyes.

I went on to tell Tim about how Peter used to play a lot of chess and how eventually no one in town could play with him anymore because he just got too good at it.  I told your Timothy how Peter then started watching a lot of golf on television and how he sent away for maps and pictures and scorecards of the best golf courses and then played those courses in his head.  Come to think of it, I think I forgot to tell you how much Peter's collection has grown ever since he got high speed internet.  Your Timothy didn't bother to experience any of that.

That's not the worst of it.  Turns out that Tim was lying to me again.  I called Peter after Tim went over to that girl's house and it

120

seems that your Timothy wheeled Peter to the railing and then left him alone. He said that Tim went down on the beach and played volleyball with some other kids. Peter didn't seem to mind but it sure did destroy the whole purpose for Tim being there. I should blow my stack over being lied to again but how often is that going to work? I guess I am going to have to sleep on that one. Well good night Martha. I love you . . .

*March 8th*

~ now that was fun. I only have a minute Martha. I need to take a shower and then go meet up with Ted. We are going to drive down to Larry's new place and have a look at that big cooler he bought.

I wanted to jot down a note or two though while the day's still fresh. You know, there are times when I forget how much fun Tim and I have together. Ted pretty much had the "crowd" under control (you know I use that term loosely this time of year). Anyway, the restaurant was slow so I drove Tim out to the golf course on the pretext of having lunch. Then I talked Peter into taking us out to the driving range even though he was adamant that he could only stay with us for a little while. So there we were - me and Peter and Tim. I doubt your Timothy knew what to think of it at first.

After we warmed up I had Peter talk us through the back nine at Sawgrass - the one down in Florida. You know, the one with the island par three. I wanted to play all 18 holes but Peter insisted that he only had time for 9 holes. Well, Tim teed up first and hit a line shot straight down the middle of the driving range. Peter figured that Tim only had a nine iron left in order to reach the tenth green in two. I saw a gleam in Tim's eyes then. He had me and he knew it. He said, "Take all the practice you need Pops, I'll go get us another round." I'm here to tell you that hearing that made me nervous. I was about to pay dearly for my habit of never going to the driving range and we all knew it. All three of us. I never have gotten used to hitting off that fake plastic grass. Those practice tee boxes are pretty darn thin if you ask me. They hardly give any feel other than the stupid piece of plywood they're trying to hide. I usually end up hitting down on them too hard and slamming my club head into that plastic covered wood. Thud, thud, thud is all

121

you'd hear if I spent too much time on that driving range. Needless to say I was thinking about that and about Tim's perfect drive when I hit my first shot off the little rubber tee that sticks out of that fake plastic grass. Well, I hooked that first shot just as Tim was walking up the slope from the clubhouse. I thought about asking Peter for a Mulligan but I didn't. I thought I'd just try and relax a little while Tim hit his second shot.

I didn't get to relax. It hadn't dawned on me that I was still away so I had to hit next. I tried to place my ball for my next shot out in front of the tee box, on the real grass, but Peter wouldn't let me. Said we had to hit from the fake grass. I pulled a 5 iron out of my bag but made sure to give both Tim and Peter a look of disgust as I took a practice swing. I can still feel the pause of my back swing and the terrible gut feeling I had during my down swing just before the thud! It's a wonder I didn't break my wrist. Peter said it was because I was trying to hit down and lift up on the ball. He said I do it all the time and that I really should just let the angle of the club do the job. All I know is that I left that imaginary tenth hole two shots down by the time Peter figured I was close enough to putt out.

Our game went on like that for a while. Peter would begin each hole by describing it to us in every detail. From tee to green. Peter would describe how wide the fairway was and how far it was to the first impediment like a sand trap or a bend in the trees. He would even point out markers on the driving range in order to help us get a visual image of where our next shot should go. For example, on one hole a big white 100 yard sign might mark where a bunker would be on the real Sawgrass course. Or, one of the orange flags that Peter uses to mark his sprinkler heads might represent where a fairway makes a sharp bend to the right or left.

Tim and I learned real quick too that we had better listen to what Peter was telling us. If he said that there was a tree limb in our way ten yards ahead and then we hit a shot that he thought might have hit that limb - well. Let's just say that your actual ball might have gone two hundred yards down the driving range but in Peter's mind it hit that tree limb and only went 60 yards. And by god that's how you played it - period. I think we were on about the 14th hole when Tim finally lost his ability to drive the ball straight. I don't think he can handle his beer as well as he thinks he can. It's still a miracle though that I was only five shots back by the time we reached the 17th tee.

*That's when Tim got cocky. According to Peter, Tim's tee shot hit on the back side of the green but then it did a two hop bounce into the water. Ha! Boy, did your Timothy argue that one. By the time I came back with another round of beer Tim was still fighting Peter's call. Well he should have used that time to calm down because Peter had his drop shot land in the water too. I went to the 18th tee only one shot back. One shot Martha! Still lost though. But, God, that was fun.*

*You know I never realized that Tim didn't know how Peter ended up owning the golf course. Your little Timothy didn't even know that Peter designed our little hometown course. No he didn't. I'm telling you we split a pizza in the clubhouse after and that boy had no idea how John had gotten us all together in a secret meeting and how we hatched a plan to form a co-op in order to buy the land so Peter could make us a golf course. I guess that was a long time ago. Hell, I guess it's been three years ago that Peter finally bought us all out. Owns the whole thing now. You know that though. Remember we all got so drunk you had to pick us up that night and taxi everyone home? You even carried Peter into his house because you'd been too damn mad to mess with his wheelchair. You remember that night Martha? How much can you remember? I often find myself wondering about that.*

*I was feeling so good about our day that I slipped up and got a little too pious with Tim. At least I think I did. Not too much though. We were both a little tipsy and I told Tim that old joke about Beethoven. Do you remember that one? How Beethoven gets to heaven and is rewarded for having such a good life by being allowed to ask God one question? Well, old egotistical Beethoven wasted his one question by asking God who was the greatest composer of all time and God replies, "Steven Smith." Then Beethoven says he never heard of any Steven Smith and God replies, "that's because he never got a chance to play."*

*How come you're not laughing? You used to laugh at that one. Don't worry, your Timothy didn't get it either. I waited all these years for that boy to be old enough for us to get drunk together and he doesn't even chuckle at that one. Maybe I told it wrong? Actually, now that I think about it, maybe this time that story had meaning and Tim didn't think I was joking. Maybe he didn't laugh because he understood, like I am starting too, that I was really talking about Peter and golf. We sure had fun though. Well I'd best get a shower.*

*. . . I'm back Martha. Guess I'll turn in early tonight. I have a meeting up to Bangor in the morning. I'm going to try and get us some better pricing on beef. Good night Martha. I love you. Tim loves you too, you know that right?*

*Good evening Martha,*

*I have a little bit of an update on Timothy but first I really, really need to tell you about my morning. You're never going to believe this one. It's been a while since I felt so alive. And so stupid too. We could have all gotten arrested.*

*I was driving the side roads back from Bangor and there was this whole line of cars parked alongside the road. Actually, a lot of them were still partly on the road so I had to drive slow. At one point I was only doing three miles an hour. I know - I looked. I was starting to get a little ticked too. I only took the back road so I could relax a little. Well this one guy was walking back to his car so I asked him what was going on and he said that a group of people had caught this moose and they were trying to load it into a trailer.*

*I had to see that for myself so I found a place to pull over and walked up to the crowd. There was this big circle of people around what looked to be a '62 Cadillac with this beat up rental trailer hooked to it. The doors of the trailer were swung wide open with this makeshift ramp made up from two long boards sticking out of it. I didn't see the moose at first. Then there it was - running around in the center of all those people half scared out of its mind.*

*I asked this one lady what was going on and she said that these two hippies had hit the moose with the Cadillac and it kind of started to limp away so they got the idea to load it into their trailer and take it home. One guy thought that they planned on using some old Native American remedy to heal the poor thing but another lady said that they were going to butcher it and share the meat with everybody who helped. Said that was the only reason she was helping.*

*Well I tell you about that time the moose took a run at the trunk of that rusty old Cadillac and somehow got itself up on the roof. We were all coming up with different plans on how to get it down when the State Police showed up. Sure put a pisser on the whole deal. I thought about getting the heck out of there but this one* really big officer told us to all stay put until he could figure out what was going on. I spent the next couple of minutes really thinking hard about making up a story - that I had only just gotten there and didn't know anything. Then I looked at my shoes and they were all covered in mud from when I ran out into the grass when we all thought the moose was going to break out into the field. That plus the bottom of my pants had turned damn near bright green from the wet grass and weeds. I really didn't have much choice other than to hang around and prepare to tell the truth. You know it turns out that those hippies hadn't hit that moose at all. It was standing in the middle of the road and they just got it in their stoned little heads to take the thing home as a pet. I tell you - some people's kids!

Sure was fun while it lasted though. Well, good night Martha. Oh, I forgot to tell you about Tim. Sorry about that. Seems that Tim didn't learn anything yesterday at all. I stopped by the restaurant on the way home to help with the books and it's also about time I really gave that grill a good cleaning. Right away Ted proceeded to inform me about how your Timothy had sent Nancy home at nine o'clock. She's the new little waitress I told you about last month. Tiny little thing. Well Tim sent her home and took over her station so he could get some tip money. Then he had the gall to leave Ted short-handed around 11 o'clock so he could take that girl of his to some damn concert.

I tell you Martha he just doesn't understand does he! These people have families damn it! I'm going to have to say good night Martha. I'm getting pissed just thinking about what your boy did today. Well, good night anyway.


*March 10th*

Martha,

Well it's the end of another day and I am still wrestling with what to do about Tim. He didn't show up for work until after two this afternoon. He's been around that place long enough to know we're only busy from 7:30 in the morning until around noon this time of year. What the hell good does it do for him to show up at two? I know. I know. Stop cursing. But damn it all. I don't know what to do. I don't know what will get to that boy. What's going to make him grow up? You tell me and I'll do it.

*I never felt this helpless as a parent before. Am I even supposed to care anymore? I mean the boy is old enough that I shouldn't even care, right? I'm at a loss. I am sitting here and there's nothing at all in the front, middle or even in the back of my brain Martha. Nothing. Maybe Peter was the wrong guy. Maybe Tim really can't see past Pete's wheelchair. Maybe I should have had Timothy spend some time with Paul. I should give him a call before it gets too late. Be back in a minute. Now that the kid isn't in school anymore, it might do him some good to get to know Paul as an adult. He should know how much of an inspiration Paul can be. Okay, I'd better go call if I am going to . . .*

*. . . Paul said he'd do it. He said he'd take some time off and take the kid hiking in the morning if I thought that might help. In the morning. Right away. Now that's Paul for you. I hope it does Tim some good. If anyone is going to get to that kid it's going to be Paul. Do you remember the first time we ever saw him? It was at that school board meeting years ago. I think you and I went to that. Or did we just hear about it so much I'm remembering we went to it? Remember all the fuss? Paul was this up and coming superstar football coach and they were going to create a new position in the social studies department at the high school so they could hire him away from that big school up in Bangor. Remember that? I think that was the last time the whole town turned up for a school board meeting. If I am remembering right we were split three ways. One side didn't think we needed a new football coach as much as we needed better education for our kids. One side thought that a winning football team would give a boost to all of the kids and then the school as a whole would improve. The third side just didn't give a shit - we just went to see a fight. Got one too.*

*Marge Petersen, I think it was. Wasn't she the one who kept yelling that she wanted a chance to be heard. That she didn't care about no damn list. Now I remember. We did go to that meeting. Anyway, remember how Marge went up to the school board chairman, took his gavel right out of his hand and threw it out the window? I can still hear the dead silence when that glass shattered. Then Hank yelled out something like, "with an arm like that, let's just make Ms. Petersen the coach." I thought sure she'd beat Hank to death for saying that but she didn't. Good old Marge just lumped Hank in with the rest of us. Let us all have it. She went on and on about how we only had one foreign language teacher trying to* teach both French and Spanish and how we didn't even have an art department.

That's when Paul stood up. He was in the back row the whole damn time and no one even knew it. He sure showed us what class was that night. Don't you think so Martha? I think he made everyone feel about two feet tall by the time he finished speaking. I know I felt like crap and I was one of those who just went for the spectacle. Remember how Paul stood up straight as a board and apologized for causing so much turmoil? I think he said turmoil. That really stands out in my mind for some reason. Anyway, his point was that he didn't want to be the cause of so much turmoil in a community that he had really hoped to become a part of. Remember how he promised to pay for the broken window? Remember that! He promised to pay for that window and then he turned to Marge and said, "Ms. Petersen is correct. Education should be your first priority and I am not willing to be a detriment to the bettering of your children. I really want to live here and be your coach but not like this. So I'll make you a deal Ms. Petersen. I'll stay where I am for now and go to night school to get certified to teach Spanish. Then, if you still want me, I'll come coach your team." That's exactly what he did. We hired him as a Spanish teacher one year to the day later.

It might do Tim good to spend some time with a guy like Paul. Sure can't hurt. It's getting late Martha. I should think about going to bed. I love you. . .


*March 11th*

Dear Martha,

I was just now thinking that this might actually be the first night I cooked and ate in this house since you left . . .

I can't really describe how I feel about that. Not the eating part - food's just food anymore to me. The odd part is how I feel, or don't feel, about the revelation I just had about the lack of your presence. It feels strange to have been just sitting here and then finding myself thinking about myself and not really about you. That's the revelation I think. I found myself having to conjure up the feeling of missing you. Odd. I guess I've been wrapped up in odd thoughts all day.

I went to the golf course for lunch and got to talking to Peter and the next thing you know it was three o'clock before I realized I *hadn't eaten. Guess I hadn't been too hungry anyway. Got wrapped up in talking with Peter too much maybe. I did learn something. There is that, I suppose. Every time I think I know all there is to know about Paul, there's more. I should know better by now.*

*I'm telling you that what Peter told me today really makes sense. Now that I am sitting here thinking about it all over again it really makes sense. I must admit though that Peter's initial statements about Paul correcting and improving our whole community seemed a bit much at first. Maybe I haven't been a good listener over the years because Peter claims we had the same talk a few years ago. Is he right? Was I not a good listener? Well I listened today, that's for sure. I was a bit skeptical though. After all, how much of an impact can one high school football coach have? Quite a bit it turns out. Leave it to Peter to think these things through.*

*It appears that Paul was considered to be more than a little odd in his coaching style the first couple of years he was here. He watched game films on Sunday like most coaches but that's where the similarities ended. Paul went over his findings with his assistants and the team on Mondays and then together they would come up with a practice schedule for the upcoming game on Friday. Together means everyone Martha: players, coaches, the equipment manager and even the trainers all had a say on what went right or wrong. Everyone had an equal say as to how to fix the problems they had the previous week. That's not even the odd part. The odd part is that once Paul had the weekly ball rolling he wouldn't even show up for Tuesday's practice. He spent his Tuesdays over at the pee-wee field watching those teams practice. He was getting to know all the kids. He would only show up to actually coach his own team on Wednesdays and Thursdays.*

*Of course on Fridays we'd have a game; but, if it was a home game then Paul would spend an hour or so at the junior high school's football practice. Peter says that Paul always made sure to go to their games on Saturdays too. He went every Saturday - even to the away games.*

*So what's the point of all this? Well, I'll tell you. It wasn't long before Paul started sort of a drafting system. He got really involved. He knew which kids progressed through all those lower levels and by the time they were ready for high school he had his Famous 5. Do you remember reading about Paul's Famous 5 every year in late May? Five kids coming up from the junior high were awarded* an automatic spot on the varsity team based solely on Paul's impressions of them over the years. Of course they still had to work hard to get and keep a starting position but they spent that whole first summer without a lot of stress. They knew they had already made the varsity team while everyone else had to try out. Even some of the returning juniors and seniors, who Paul thought had lost their drive the previous fall, had to try out again.

So why does this matter? You were wondering, right? Well I was too. According to Peter it really changed the culture of the younger kids. They started trying harder not only on the football field but in other things too. They started doing better in school and staying away from things like drugs and alcohol because they didn't want to risk not being picked as one of Paul's Famous 5. I guess that's why it only took Paul seven years to bring us our first real chance at a state title. We lost that first title game remember? Got one two years later though. That was a fun fall season - wasn't it? Do you remember how the Chamber voted to have all the shops decorated with school colors and and how we were supposed to put up something new after each victory? The whole town was black and orange by the time we went to regionals. That was fun.

Well I'm rambling too much. I'm afraid I'm going to end up forgetting to tell you the important part of all this. It seems that after a few years the high school baseball coach - I think it was still Chet Ritter back then. Anyway, Peter says that Mr. Ritter really began to see the value in what Paul was doing so he started the same kind of program with the baseball team. Then bam! We had all the young football and baseball players trying to fly the straight and narrow before they even got to the junior high. Pretty cool huh! It gets better. Peter says that when Paul got the promotion to Athletic Director he made all of the head coaches come up with their own systems. Boys and girls Martha. Boys and girls - just imagine the unseen impact hiring that one man has had. And to think Marge Petersen almost screwed it all up.

I was hoping Timothy would have already come home. It's getting late. I can't really write anymore. I find myself getting more and more anxious to hear how his day went with Paul. They left around 9 this morning to go hiking and rappelling over on the south side of the park. Tim should have been home hours ago. I'll write more later if he comes home. I think I'll read a little bit for now. Love you . . .

*. . . well it's almost 12:30 Martha so I guess it's really the 12th of March. I suppose that doesn't really matter, does it? Tim came in around 11 o'clock. Said he went out with some friends. I guess Coach Paul - that's what Tim calls him, Coach Paul - well Paul dropped Tim off in town about 3 and Tim "hooked up" with a few of his friends. They ended up at that dive of a bar The Rusty Nail. I don't know how they keep getting away with calling themselves a restaurant. I bet they could screw up sushi.*

*Tim said he had fun with Paul but I really don't know what they talked about - if anything. Tim just said they hiked to an outcropping of cliffs and then Paul showed him how to set ropes to rappel. I bet I never could get you to do something like that - could I? Sounds like fun. I did it once in the Army but we only practiced a few times on some wooden towers. Maybe I should talk Paul into taking me someday.*

*Well anyway, I could tell I wasn't going to get too much out of your boy so I went to my bedroom and got that picture I took of Paul last fall. Remember I told you how I decided to keep that picture even though I am sure Paul wouldn't want me showing it around? Well I got that picture and I showed it to junior. He even managed to turn away from the television long enough to give it a glimpse.*

*"Well," I said.*

*"Well what?"*

*"What'd ya think about that?"*

*"You went fishing. I'm happy for you."*

*Boy he's thickheaded isn't he. I had to literally point at that picture 3 or 4 times before he noticed that Paul didn't have no leg. Excuse me but I've had a little to drink. Well, I guess the angle of that picture is bad or maybe I just know what I'm looking for but if you look you can clearly tell that Paul's left pant leg is folded odd over the arm of his chair. If you really look you can see that his leg is missing below the knee.*

*I don't think I ever told you the whole story about how that happened but I sure told your Tim. I turned the television off and fixed us a nightcap and I settled into telling Tim what Paul told us on the boat. How when he was a junior in college he had been a star running back and had gotten drunk at a post game party one night. Maybe I told you this already? I think I told you the day after that day last fall on John's boat. Remember? That's when we all* got to play fighting and Paul and John fell overboard. Well Paul's fake leg hit the railing funny and came off and floated away. I had ahold of one of the chairs with my right hand so I didn't go over with the rest of them. I looked up fast though when I heard that odd metal on metal sound - it was just so unexpected. Good thing Paul's leg is mostly aluminum. We circled that boat around for over an hour before we found it floating in the waves.

I know. I know. I'm still amazed that you could know a guy for years and not know he has a fake leg. I never really even noticed that he always wears pants. Now that I think about it that is a little strange for a football coach. Anyway, I guess it's safe to say that the school kids had no idea about Paul's leg. Not if Tim didn't know about it. Even tonight Tim didn't know about it and they just spent a whole day hiking.

Well I told Tim the whole story about how Paul got drunk and wrecked his motorcycle and lost his leg and his football scholarship and everything. He lost everything. The way Paul told it his parents even disowned him. Said he spent about two years feeling sorry for himself before he decided to grow up and go back to school. I guess the town he first coached in knew about his leg and he just got tired of being treated different. He said he was determined that no one in our town would ever find out. We didn't either, did we. Well, except for John. It turns out that John found out a few years ago but promised not to tell anyone. Which seems silly now that I think about it. Who is going to care after all these years? Who would care after all Paul has done for us?

How would people treat him different? I mean he's not like Peter. He's fully functional. Paul must have just decided to not be known for anything but his coaching. Maybe he is still a little embarrassed for the accident having been his own fault. Still, I bet Paul must have days when he really regrets losing his leg. Wow, could you imagine? Just think of how many lives would have been different if Paul hadn't gotten into coaching. I always thought I would like to have a life like his. Wouldn't that be something to be able to look back on a long life with the pride of knowing how many people you have helped along the way? I used to think that would be the way to go. Too late for me I guess but not for Paul and not for your Timothy either if he'd just wake up.

I could tell that Timothy was more than a little impressed by the whole deal but I don't think he really got the big picture. He didn't focus in on the fact that Paul decided upon a certain course of life

*and through sure will and determination he made it happen. I don't
think Timothy understood that part at all. Now Paul's going to get
pissed at me for letting that cat out of the bag. Well there's nothing
I can do about it now. It's really late Martha. I should think about
getting some sleep. Good night Martha ~ I love you. You should
know that I caught Tim looking at your picture on the piano tonight.
I can tell he still loves you too . . .*

*March 12th*

*Martha,*

    *We were pretty busy this morning. I mean really busy for the
middle of March. We handled it though and I even treated Tim to a
beer after we slowed down. We met up at the clubhouse. I thought
since we hit it off there before that it would be a good place to relax
together. I wanted to try and spark some kind of conversation about
his interest and where he would like to travel - stuff like that. I got
nothing. Nothing. Am I pushing too hard Martha? I mean between
me and Peter and Paul? Is it too overboard?*

    *I hope not because John came by our table right in the middle of
my fumbling around for the right thing to say. John was just being
polite but I ended up getting him caught up in this whole mess. I
didn't know that he hasn't seen Timothy since our kids played
soccer together. That was years ago. Boy, time goes by quick don't
it? Well one thing led to another and I got John to agree to show
Tim around the business world. He wants Tim to meet him at his
office in town at six tomorrow morning. Good luck is all I have to
say to that one. I suppose I'll get up and get him going. I might
even drive him down there. John's not the kind of man you make
wait around. Not anymore. Rumor is that he owns half the town
these days. I hope this works out. Your Timothy might have just
cause to have me committed if I push him any harder. Well, I had
better get some sleep so I can get that boy into a suit and out the
door in the morning. Good night Martha ~ I hope you know how
much I love you.*

*March 13th*

*Dearest Martha,*

    *I have a confession to make. I didn't go to work today. I got
Timothy up and dressed and I took him to John's office like I was*

*supposed to. I was going to go right to the restaurant but something made me hang around downtown. I felt like I had just dropped our Tim off for his first day of school and I had this inner-compulsion to hang around in case he might need me. I must have looked pretty stupid now that I think about it. I kept popping in and out of shops hoping that I might run into them.*

*I did end up meeting a nice young couple that I think you would like. Catherine was her name but I'm having a hard time remembering her husband's name. He ran off so quick I didn't really get a chance to get to know him. They bought the old clock shop and are making it over into a combination book store and coffee bar. It's coming together really nice too. They're doing it in a colonial style with some really vibrant greens and blues.*

*The first smart thing they did was to hire Jack Kelly's outfit for the carpentry work. With Jack's touch, you already know how classy that place is going to end up looking. Maybe I'll head back down there in a few weeks to give you an update. I guess it really is spring after all isn't it Martha. It seems that every year somebody's dream is ending while someone else's is just beginning. You remember how my theory is that the only ones making out around here are the painters and the carpenters. Well, anyway, I wished her luck and walked up to Larry's new Italian restaurant for lunch. Thought what the hell - I'm here. Guess who came in two seconds after me? No, not Timothy and John. Just John.*

*He actually had to ask to join me for lunch. John shouldn't have felt he needed to ask such a question. Why would he have thought otherwise? I can only imagine what the expression on my face might have been when John came through Larry's front door alone. I finally worked up the nerve to ask him where Tim was while we waited to get seated. It must have seemed odd to John that I waited so long to ask such an obvious question. I really was nervous. When I saw John walk through that door alone I immediately thought that your kid had done something really stupid to piss him off. John just said, "On a Lobster boat. Probably circling around and bringing in the traps by now."*

*"Huh." That's all I said. It took me a few more seconds to manage to ask him why a lobster boat? He told me that Tim needs to realize that lobster is the only real industry we have in this town. Said if Tim is going to stick around here then he had better learn at least that. Then we talked about the lobster business and a lot of different things while we ate. There's too much to repeat here. I*

*missed a great deal of it anyway. I just kept thinking about our Tim on a lobster boat. In one of my business suits no less. John is right though. It might do the kid some good to realize that tourism could drop to nothing and then this town is going to sink or swim on the lobster business alone. I guess John is pretty smart after all.*

*Do you remember when he first bought the McDonald's franchise? Remember how much we worried that our business would drop by having a McDonald's go in just two blocks down. Do you remember Martha? I know I was scared. Timothy had just started grade school and you were pregnant again. All I could think about was the restaurant going under. We didn't know you would lose that baby. We didn't know that yet. Remember that's the day you slapped me in the car. I remember that now like it was five minutes ago. You swung your left hand around so fast you nearly broke my nose with your knuckles. I can see it all over again now. We were driving by the construction site and John was standing on a big mound of dirt with blueprints in his hand and I said something to the effect that we didn't have to worry because John was dumber than the pile of dirt he was standing on. God, you really hit me hard. Didn't talk to me for a week after that either, as I recall.*

*I knew a different John than you did back then. John was a good hand on the boats and a good fella to hang around with at the pubs but I tell you he couldn't add 2 + 2 without coming up with 3.8 or something. Well he couldn't. Bet he still can't. Who knew he had saved all that money though? Who knew? Those McDonald's people told him to stick to there regimen and he would do fine and you know he did just that. He did exactly what they told him to do and the next thing you know he's bringing a franchised hotel to town. John just did what they told him to do too. Now look at him. He owns near half the town. Well good for him.*

*Anyway, our little Timothy was too tapped out to talk about his day when he came home. I don't think he will be applying for a job on one of those boats anytime soon. He did say that John promised to show him around for real tomorrow. He's going to introduce Tim to some other business owners. I'm hoping that Tim might start to get the picture that there are more opportunities in life than just the restaurant business. Well good night Martha. I'll be thinking about you. Love you . . .*

Martha,

I tell you I never wanted to be a fly on the wall any more than I wanted to today. My whole day was just one big lump of anticipation. And then what a let down. Tim just left to go see that girl again. I tell you I don't know how I feel right now. That boy was only home long enough to get changed. I tried to spark a conversation about his day with John but I am starting to realize that I am not really any good at that. As far as I can tell, it appears that John did everything he could to give Tim a one day education in business. I really can't see that it did any good.

Tim told me that John took him by his hotel to have breakfast with the hotel manager. I suppose that the manager was there to talk to Tim about running a hotel but all Tim could tell me was that she was cute and single. That's it! Cute and single. After breakfast they went into town and John spent the rest of the day introducing our Tim to the various shop owners that he is partners with. You know what your Tim got out of that? Let me get a drink and I'll try and tell you what your Timothy got from that . . .

. . . where were we? Oh yes, your dumb ass son. You know what he told me? I was following him around the house trying to get something out of him about his day with John while he looked for his shoes. You know what he took from it? He thinks that all those people he met today had only one thing in common - John. Tim thinks that none of those people would be in business if it weren't for John so the only lesson he got was to sit around on his ass some more and wait for someone to give him everything. How stupid can he be. He didn't even take time to note the hardships those people went through. He doesn't want to see that they worked damn hard to develop the skills and talents that led John to invest in them . . .

. . . sorry about that Martha. I went to get another drink. No, I'm not drinking too much. It was your Tim who missed the hole so let's not change the subject. Sure John helped some people get started with business loans and all. Sure John is still part owner in some of those businesses but John never once invested in a tee shirt shop or gift store. Never once. John invested in people. They were all hard working people who had proved their metal before John ever got involved. Oh, why am I telling you. You know all this. It's like Tim is with our place. The kid never would take the time to learn about inventory or pricing structures. He won't even meet with the vendors let alone learn how to negotiate better pricing so *that we might have a little profit. I'll bet he doesn't even realize that on most days the waitstaff clears more money in tips than we do. I have to admit that it is a little easier now that the building and equipment are paid off. But still . . .*

*I don't know Martha. I just don't know . . .*

*I tried to tell Tim how John's parents had raised him hard. I told your Timothy how John's parents had taken him out of school and how they had put him to work on the boats when he was only 13. I told that boy of yours how John's parents somehow knew that it was his only hope. Since the first grade John's parents had been told that he was only being passed along for social reasons. John was out on them boats before he even reached the junior high school. His parents could no longer take the ridicule their son had to endure.*

*I thought everybody in town knew John's story. Not your boy. He acted like it was news to him when I told him how John's parents took him out of school and put him to work and taught him how to save money. That's just what John did too. Word is that he worked the boats by day and washed dishes at The Rusty Nail at night. And now John looks for that in people. He respects hard work and rewards it. I guess I was hoping Tim would get that message.*

*Guess I'm going to have to find someway to thank John even if it didn't do any good. Well Martha there's not much more to write about. It seems my mind has been too wrapped up in helping Tim lately. Am I too involved? Should I just let it go and give him a job and a home? Just let him figure it all out for himself? Let me think about it. I really don't know what the right thing to do is. I wish you were here to help me. I bet if you were here I wouldn't have even bothered Peter or Paul or John with this stuff. This should be a family thing, right? I need to sleep on it. Maybe I'll take a road trip tomorrow. Maybe I just need some distance. Well good night Martha. I love you . . .*

*March 15th*

*Martha,*

*Well I got a false start on my little road trip today. I had thoughts of going up to North Point even though it's Ted's day off. I had it set in my mind that your Timothy could open the store. I figured there wasn't any reason why Tim couldn't do the cooking today. If he's going to eat and sleep on my dime then he needs to do something. Right? I had even just thought of turning off my cell phone when Nancy called and told me she couldn't get in the restaurant. Seems your boy didn't show up.*

*No problem. I thought I'd just swing by and let Nancy in and the next thing you know it's eight o'clock. And then it's 8:30 and still no Tim. He rolled in at exactly 8:43. Said it wasn't his job to open up. Well I told him to just keep right on walking. Told him not to come back either. I was so mad. You know what he said? Said he didn't care. Said that if I didn't want him then his friend Mark could get him hired on at The Rusty. The Rusty Martha. Are you believing that? Bullshit's what I say to that. It would just be another stop over for him while he waits around for me to give him our place. He's using our restaurant as a crutch. I'm telling you he is. Well he is.*

*I'm going out Martha. I thought I'd write you early because I'm planning on getting good and drunk tonight. Ted promised to stop by and take me with him to his bowling league. I am too going to get drunk. Then I'm going to forget about this whole mess. Then I'm going to sleep it off until God knows what hour and I am going on that road trip. Anyway, here's to an early good night. That's right. I already poured myself a drink. Good night Martha ~ love you.*

*March 16th*

*Martha I am a fool. A living, breathing fool. How can a person live this many years two miles from the sea and forget what it smells like, what it sounds like? I cook with salt every day and yet there is no smell to match it when it rides in on a wave of moisture. It seems that the gulls have kept their cadence as well. They still rise and fall in concert with the sounds of the surf on the rocks. It all still flows doesn't it.*

*Oh Martha, how much did we miss? How little did we live? I sat there on those rocks for hours and not once did I think about Tim or the restaurant. I ended up thinking that maybe these past few weeks didn't have anything to do with Tim at all. Maybe I'm the one who needs a change?*

*We both came to this spot - this speck on the map - from very different paths didn't we Martha. Maybe I need to move on. I don't know. Am I using Tim as my own excuse not to grow? Is the*

137

*restaurant his crutch or mine? I've been away from there a lot lately. Ted seems to be doing just fine. Just fine. Maybe I'm the one who should take a lesson from John. What did I write the other day? That John invests in people? Well isn't Ted worth investing in? Let me sleep on it Martha. I must say I haven't been this calm, this relaxed in years. Well, good night Martha. Please know I love you. No matter what happens Martha, I love you . . .*

*March 17th*

*Dear Martha,*

 *Well I did it. I took the leap Martha. I called Henry as soon as his office opened and he agreed to meet me for lunch at the restaurant. It didn't take long to work out all of the details and Henry seems to think that he can have the final paperwork in place in a week or two . . .*

 *A week or two! Just think of it Martha - puff, gone - in just a week or two. All those years gone . . .*

 *Well I'm not going to look back. I'm selling this place to Ted and that's that. I think it will do the place some good. Ted must have pointed out thirty things he wanted to fix or paint or get rid of while he was still sitting here with Henry and me. There we were trying to figure out how to get this thing done and Ted's mind was already redecorating and replacing things. I tried to put the brakes on his enthusiasm but I tell you there was no cooling him off. I said, "Ted you can't spend all that money before you earn it." I told him, "you still have to pay for the place you know." Well get this Martha - he has the money. Turns out that Ted's been saving up for years to buy his own restaurant. I asked him why he never approached me about buying our place. Said he always assumed we'd give it to Timothy. Said the whole town thinks that.*

 *Give it to Timothy? Now there's a notion. I mean really do you think we could have put all these families into his hands? That's not it though is it. Is it? No, Tim never was meant for this place any more than it was meant for him. Fact is he doesn't even know about it yet. I wonder what he is going to think? One thing is for sure - Tim won't be coming back to work here. That's for sure. Not for Ted. I think it will do your boy some good to know that every one of his future decisions have weight to them. Consequences would be a better word maybe.*

*I tell you Martha I see your boy sticking out this season at The Rusty but I bet he moves on next winter when this whole town goes dead again. I'll even bet you a dollar that that girl dumps him too once she figures out that he's not going to inherit this place. You might as well put that dollar in my pocket. I already have it spent. No Martha, I tell you that boy won't be around come next spring. Wonder if I will? No sense thinking too far ahead but maybe I should do some traveling myself. I don't know. One step at a time I guess.*

*You know I never realized how much I let this place go by just not noticing stuff. I'm still sitting here at the front corner table by the small window. I should get to doing something else but I can't help just sitting here and looking around. Do you remember when that punk kid with the skateboard broke off part of the leg on the back booth? I bet that was twenty years ago wasn't it? Remember how I went out to the alley and broke off piece of a pallet and shoved it under there thinking I'd fix it later? Well I tell you Martha that piece of broken pallet is still shoved up under the front outer leg of that booth. Yes Martha, Ted's going to do okay. Maybe even better than okay since he's not coming into the business second hand the way you and I did . . .*

*. . . sorry about that Martha, my mind drifted away there for a little while. Speaking of going away, I was just now thinking that I hope you don't mind that I have taken to writing these thoughts down so that I can read them to you later. I can't visit you every day like I used to. It's just too hard on me. I get to thinking of you there in the ground and me still above . . .*

*It's just too hard. I don't want to forget to tell you things though, so I'm writing them down to read them to you when I get there. I can even leave these letters by your stone if you would like?*

*Don't cry Martha. Tim will be all right even if he does end up leaving town. I know. I know. I'm going to miss him too. But he's a strong boy. He'll be all right. He doesn't know it yet. But he's a strong boy. I love you too Martha. Please don't be angry with me. Our Timothy will be alright. I know you love him but please stop crying. I am going to miss him too . . .*

*. . . I'm going to have to say good bye for now Martha. I don't really have it in me to write more today. God, how often I pray that it is still possible for you to know how much I love you. Please stop crying; you know I could never walk away when you were crying.*